Cail, Carol.

If two of the
dead.

$21.95

DATE			

...

IF TWO
OF THEM
ARE DEAD

...

Also featuring Maxey Burnell

Private Lies
Unsafe Keeping

···
IF TWO
OF THEM
ARE DEAD
···

Carol Cail

A THOMAS DUNNE BOOK

St. Martin's Press ❧ New York

A THOMAS DUNNE BOOK.
An imprint of St. Martin's Press.

Library of Congress Cataloging-in-Publication Data

Cail, Carol.
    If two of them are dead : a Maxey Burnell mystery / by Carol Cail.—1st ed.
        p.   cm.
    "A Thomas Dunne Book."
    ISBN 0–312–14361–3
    1. Women journalists—Colorado—Boulder—Fiction. 2. Boulder (Colo.)—Fiction. I. Title.
PS3553.A385I3   1996
813'.54—dc20   96–6988
                                                                      CIP

First Edition: July 1996

10   9   8   7   6   5   4   3   2   1

This one's dedicated with great affection to Becky,
who drives a Formula V.

IF TWO
OF THEM
ARE DEAD

"Are you serious? You are serious. Oh God, you're
going to leave me alone here?"

At least he'd waited till Thursday to break the news—till the
paper was in the can, or, more accurately, in the racks, in the mail,
and in the hands of its several thousand readers. This way, she
could devote her full attention to the horrible problem of his deserting her.

"Pull yourself together, Burnell. Don't be a crybaby," he snarled,
to shame her into remembering her independence, her pride, her
tough streak.

But at the moment, Maxey felt worse than when they'd agreed
to a divorce, more than three years ago. Of course, then she'd been
the leaver and Reece had been the leave-ee. Then the pain had been
a dull ache in her chest. Now she felt as if she had inadvertently
boarded a roller coaster and hung poised on the first awful peak, the
path before her a rickety jumble of wooden planks. How could she
hope to navigate the ups and downs without Reece?

She felt behind herself for the nearest of their assorted office chairs and sank into it, still staring at her ex-husband. He, in contrast, stood straight as a cadet called on the carpet, blue eyes intent on the far wall, every line of his lean body exuding determination, only his Opus the Penguin T-shirt giving away his true nature.

"What would Jim say?" Maxey made an effort not to whine. "He wouldn't have willed the newspaper to us if he'd thought we'd just curl up and quit."

"Old Jim would be surprised and pleased that I lasted this long," Reece said, looking directly at her now, scowling at her. "He knew me. He knew I'm not the kind to plod myself into a rut."

"Where will you go?" It was an automatic question, with no relevance whatever to the discussion. Whether he went to Tibet or to the next town up the road made no difference. The result would be the same. She would be the sole captain of the *Blatant Regard,* Colorado's most outspoken weekly newspaper, a rowboat in a sea of battleship dailies.

"I've always wanted to go to Alaska," Reece said. His posture relaxed a notch. "Go up there and look around at least, see what the opportunities might be for—"

"I can't buy you out. I don't have the money."

Reece smiled. "You don't have to buy me out. I've got a buyer."

"A buyer." Her dismay compounded with interest. "A woman. Oh, Reece, you aren't going to saddle me with one of your floozy girlfriends!"

"No, as delightful as that sounds. He's a man. You're going to love him. Guy by the name of Clark Dumpty."

"You're kidding."

"Nope, that's it. Clark—"

"You can't sell to somebody with a name like that. How's it going to look on the masthead?"

"Come on, Maxey. You don't judge people by their names. Where's that smart, adventurous, open-minded woman—"

"Has this noodlehead signed anything yet? Have you got his money?"

"No, but it's all settled, Maxey."

"Why didn't you discuss it with me first? This is so unfair." She slapped the arm of the chair and then clutched her stinging fingers to her chest.

Reece rolled his eyes. "I've been telling you I wanted to sell my half, almost since the day we got the *Regard*."

"You were kidding. I thought you were kidding."

Reece crossed to her and squatted down, a hand on either arm of her chair, gazing up into her face. He hadn't looked at her like this, so earnest and caring, since the day before she found him in flagrante delicto with their then neighbor, Libby Rae Fitz.

"Maxey," he said. "Give Clark a chance. I know you're going to like him if you just give him half a chance. Wait till you meet him before you make up your mind to hate him."

"All right." She folded her arms and stared back, eye for eye, but hers were cold. "When?"

"The sooner the better. How about tonight? Dinner at Rev Taylor's? I'll buy."

Maxey knew at that moment she was doomed. If Reece was willing to buy at anywhere other than McDonald's, he must be truly desperate to leave the *Regard*.

■

She left work early, though not as early as Reece. As she stepped outside, the dry summer air closed around her like a warming oven. Along the brick mall, the petunias in their lamppost baskets looked like tongues hanging out.

While Maxey locked the office door, pedestrians trooped up and down Pearl Street, most of them young and dressed in nineties grunge or sixties leftovers. The bongo busker occupied his usual acoustical spot, the glassed-in bus stop. Prospective passengers stood outside and smiled or frowned, depending on their enthusiasm for drumming.

Maxey set off in the opposite direction, sidestepping a toddler who struggled to subdue a yellow balloon roughly the same size and shape as he. Passing the Dilly Deli, Maxey waved, in case her friend Morrie was in there looking out. She paused at the Banana Republic window to admire a tan-and-gray tattersall shirt, then hustled across Thirteenth Street with the light.

She had walked to work today. It was seven blocks, good for her health, and left a precious parking space downtown for someone else.

Cutting north to Spruce Street, she thought about what to wear tonight: a suit, in spite of the temperature—to appear businesslike and professional and to show up Reece, who'd no doubt change his Opus shirt for a more formal, plain white T-shirt.

At the pastel green house on the corner of her block, a neighbor lady Maxey didn't know by name lifted one hand in languid greeting, her porch swing never breaking stride. Maxey waved and shrank away from a kid on a skateboard. His graceful stance and serene face indicated he felt in control as he shot the broken sidewalk rapids.

She arrived at her destination, a white Queen Anne perched on a modest slope of hard-to-mow grass, surrounded by Maxey's dead landlady's perennials. Maxey's live landlady, who'd inherited flowers and all, lived in Florida and couldn't be bothered with little details like flowers, grass, or leaky plumbing, so Maxey and the downstairs tenant, a nice elderly gentleman named Ollie Kraig, divided up the maintenance duties and subtracted them from the rent. To date, there had been no complaints from Jacksonville about their rates.

Maxey clanked open the black mailbox next to her door and prized out three envelopes. She let herself into the stairwell and trooped up to her apartment.

"Hello, honey, I'm home," she called ahead.

Sometimes she locked the door at the top; sometimes she didn't.

This time, she hadn't. It swung open on her combination living room/kitchen, where her roommate, Moe the cat, waited for supper, his irritation visible in the switching of his gray tail.

"You have to eat alone tonight," Maxey said, spooning a glob of pungent cat food out of a can bearing Moe's spitting image. "Okay if I don't light the candles?"

Ignoring her, Moe dug in. Watching him, Maxey felt renewed anxiety cramp her stomach. Like the *Regard*, Moe had been left to her by Jim Donovan. At least Moe wouldn't quit her to go tomcatting off to Alaska.

She fanned out the three envelopes that she'd dropped on the counter beside the sink—Visa bill, phone bill, greeting card. Oh God—already? Backing a step, she consulted the Far Side calendar magnetized to the refrigerator door. August twenty-seventh was tomorrow. Maxey had about six hours left to be twenty-something.

She headed for the bathroom to check herself out in the mirror of the medicine cabinet. No wrinkles except the laughing kind. No silver hairs among the gold—this after the five-minute inspection involving a hand mirror, a magnifying glass, and lots of pawing through the roots. She wadded her hair into a ball behind her head and considered getting a serious cut. Something Princess Di–ish.

Finally, she strolled back to the kitchen and opened her birthday card from the only person in the world who would send her one. The front illustration bristled with flowers and ribbons and bluebirds and lace. Inside, the five-line sentiment rhymed. A yellow sticky note was attached. It read:

Hi, sweetie.

Happy Big Three-oh!!!

When are you going to come visit? Neither one of us is getting any younger, ha-ha.

Love
Aunt Janet.

Maxey tossed card and note into the wicker wastebasket. She'd phone Janet this weekend and they'd coo back and forth about being fine and being busy and being another year better. She liked her mother's sister, even if she couldn't dredge up love.

Moe, mellow from his fish du jour, butted Maxey's shins with his face. "Hey, buddy. Trying to seduce me? What blouse should I wear with my teal suit?"

The fat gray-and-white tabby followed her into the bedroom, leaped gracefully into the center of the unmade bed, and curled into a watchful wait as Maxey headed for the shower.

As she peeled off her work clothes, she reflected that her bio-rhythm had to be at lowest ebb—Reece betraying her, a birthday stealing her youth, Aunt Janet making her feel guilty, and, sure enough, here came her period.

■

Maxey eased her Toyota into a parking space in front of an antique shop across the street from Rev Taylor's in Niwot. No matter where she might have parked, it would have been in front of an antique shop. The little Victorian town, named for a left-handed Indian, was an antiques mecca north of Boulder.

She'd refused Reece's offer of a ride because she wanted to be able to flounce out early if this meeting went the way she expected. Looking both ways before crossing the quiet street, Maxey admired the sun backlighting a jumble of clouds above the mountains. The evening smelled of dust until she reached the flowers erupting along the picket fence of the restaurant's side yard. Their sweet and spicy fragrance followed her to the front door, where garlic and tomato took over.

Maxey paused at the brink of the long, dim room, waiting for a hostess. It was just enough time for her to study the pastries in the old-fashioned showcases and feel the saliva begin to build. The young woman who arrived with menus hugged to her bosom wore a white shirt, black walking shorts, white socks, and hiking boots. Her muscular brown legs indicated that this was not a costume.

"I'm to meet someone," Maxey said. "Reece Macy?"

"Oh, yeah, I think they're already here."

The woman strode away and Maxey followed, up a step and past mostly occupied tables, past the homey clutter of crafts and art—all with tiny white sale tags—that lay on shelves or clung to the high walls.

Maxey saw Reece and vice versa. On his best behavior, he came to his feet beside their table, an oak antique parked with the short side against the wall. He'd changed into a very nice olive plaid shirt and gray slacks. The front of the shirt still bore marks where the manufacturer had folded it.

Across from Reece, Clark Dumpty, presumably, had turned around in his chair to watch Maxey's final approach.

The hostess proceeded past the men and back toward the kitchen. Maxey longed to keep on walking right behind her.

As if reading her mind, Reece reached an arm around her shoulder and anchored her to him for the introductions. Clark, apparently of the feminist-movement generation, made no effort to stand. He smiled up at Maxey without a worry in the world or, she was afraid, a brain in his head.

Grimacing back at him, she offered her hand to be shaken. He touched it awkwardly, gripping just her fingers, though part of the reason for this was the angle of attack and the bud vase of two white carnations rearing up between.

Reece drew out the chair beside him and settled Maxey into it. She studied the layout. There was a beer stein in front of Reece, half-full, or, in her present mood, half-empty. Clark's drink looked like milk of magnesia in a brandy snifter, with a strawberry twist.

"You want a beer?" Reece asked, patting her on the shoulder before turning square in his chair and scooting toward the table.

"Okay." She snapped open her pink cloth napkin and spread it on her lap, at the ready.

"I understand you're a bit apprehensive about my investing in the *Regard*," Clark said.

Nobody smiled *all* of the time. Maybe he had some paralysis of the lips so that he couldn't shut his mouth completely. His whole face looked wider than it was long. He had plenty of straight dark hair, very little forehead, hooded eyes, a flat nose, and a strip of chin the width of a Band-Aid. If he'd fallen, like his namesake, he'd obviously landed on the top of his head.

"Tell me what your background is," Maxey said. "What qualifies you to run a newspaper?"

"Nothing." He laughed. Then he laughed again at her expression. "A desire to learn. A willingness to try anything. The cash that Reece requires."

"Ah. Uh-huh."

"He's pulling your leg, Maxey. Clark used to edit a little literary quarterly. Did it all, from acquisition to subscriptions."

"Is that so? What was the circulation?"

"Only about a hundred. Eighty, maybe. But that's good for the type 'zine it was."

"What type is that?"

"S and M. Mainly shoe fetish."

"But literary," Reece said.

"Oh, yeah. We had poetry and everything in *Worm Naked*. Got the title from a line in Chaucer."

Maxey wondered: If she burst into tears, would Clark continue to grin?

Another young woman dressed in black and white and wearing clunky shoes arrived to take Maxey's drink order.

"Have you got any whiskey?"

Reece twisted to look at her.

"No, wait. I'm driving. Iced tea."

"I'm perfectly harmless, Ms. Burnell," Clark said when the waitress bustled away. "And I assure you that you will have all the freedom you've enjoyed in the past to run the newspaper as you see fit."

"You'd be a silent partner?" That might not be so bad. Take his money and not let him have a key to the door.

"Not exactly silent." He sipped his pink swampy drink and set the snifter down. The smile, mercifully, died. "Shall we say . . . muted?"

"You can hire the help we've always wanted," Reece interjected.

Maxey suppressed a shudder, her usual reaction to remembering their one experience with an office helper, a young man who'd failed at almost everything in life except the leaving of it.

The waitress returned with the tea. "What'll it be, folks?" She looked at Maxey.

"Prime rib, baked potato, poppy-seed dressing on the salad. Bring me some fried mushrooms, too. And I'll want dessert."

Reece squirmed but said nothing.

"Sounds good," Clark said. "Bring me the same."

The girl looked at Reece. He hesitated, and Maxey guessed he was going to go with his usual—the cheapest item on the menu, whatever it might be.

"Make it a triple," he said, grinning triumphantly at Maxey. "Except I'll share Maxey's mushrooms."

"Which way is the rest room?" Clark asked the waitress as she turned away. She hand-signaled and said he couldn't miss it.

It took a moment for him to scrape back his chair as he fumbled under the table for what proved to be an aluminum cane or crutch. It fit into his palm and rose to brace his forearm. Maxey always associated such devices with polio.

"Polio," Clark said, reminding her it was impolite to stare. He limped in the designated direction, and—bad manners or not—she watched him walk out of sight.

Taller than his posture at the table had led her to believe, he was burly above and wasted below, an inverted pear. Like Maxey, he'd worn a suit—brown, with an accordion of wrinkles up the back of the jacket. His cordovan loafers needed a shine and new heels. Maybe in Clark's circle, that was sexy.

"You sure his check won't bounce?" Maxey asked Reece across the rim of her water glass.

"He lives on Mapleton Hill. Owns his mansion and another one next door. His folks had a molybdenum mine northwest of Climax in the mid-twenties."

"So the *Regard* is just an amusement. Something for him to dabble in," Maxey said bitterly.

"His business experience will be invaluable. And he really does know how to write. Ask him for a sample copy of *Worm Naked.* If you like rubber boots, I recommend the 1992 summer issue."

Maxey laughed in spite of herself. "Oh, Reece," she said, butting his shoulder with her forehead, much the way Moe had showed affection for her earlier. "I hate to admit it, but I will miss you."

"Does this mean you're ready to accept Clark?"

"I didn't say that. What if I could come up with the necessary purchase price?"

"Where would you get it?"

She shrugged. "Borrow it from the bank? Maybe from a friend or a relative?"

Reece smirked at her to demonstrate he knew as well as she did that she was talking smoke. The bank would need collateral more enticing than the flimsy assets of the *Regard.* And Maxey didn't have any friends or relatives—at least not ones with money to spare.

"Okay, forget that. Maybe I can find my own partner to buy your share."

"Darlin', I've been searching for a solid year for someone. They either have the money or the talent, but not both at the same time. Clark is the first and only investor I found that I'd trust to take the torch from me."

Maxey mouthed a crude sound. "You faker. Selling some rube your so-called half of the business, when you know damn well I'm responsible for two-thirds of the production."

"Yeah, you do work too hard." Reece dropped his arm around her shoulders. "Which leads me to the surprise."

She groaned. Reece's surprises usually required the recipient's being a good sport.

"No, listen." He gave her a quick bone-grinding squeeze. "You're going to love this. Before I leave, I'm giving you a two-week vacation."

"Unpaid, I assume." She pushed him away from her and tugged at the hem of the teal jacket, afraid that it was acquiring some accordion wrinkles of its own.

"No, no. Time off, and you draw your usual salary."

She leaned her back against the wall, mouth crooked up on one side to show weary skepticism.

At the far end of the room, Clark Dumpty appeared and began to work his way back to them. He paused to speak to a family in a booth, and whatever he said drew real laughter from the kids.

"So where do you want to go, Maxey?" Reece prompted.

"I've always wanted to see Alaska. At least take a look around and see what opportunities there might be for—"

"No, seriously. Where do you want to go?"

She opened her mouth to say nowhere, that there was nowhere she wanted to go and she didn't need a vacation from the newspaper she loved. What came out was, "Nebraska."

Reece looked as surprised as she felt, before relief at her seeming acceptance of his gift spread across his face in a grin. "Great idea. Go visit your roots."

"I'm back, kids. Should my ears have been burning?" Clark eased himself into the high-backed oak chair and stowed the crutch under it.

"We were discussing the vacation Maxey's about to take."

"Oh? Someplace exciting?"

Maxey shook her head as their waitress thumped a salad on the table in front of her. It was an interesting jumble of greens, sprouts, red cabbage, carrots, beets, cucumbers, tomatoes, hard-boiled egg, grated cheese, and a sunflower-seed garnish. She couldn't see any bits of kitchen sink.

"Nebraska," Reece said.

"The Cornhusker State, huh?" Clark cut into his salad with his knife and fork.

Maxey didn't know why his smile irritated her so much. Would she have preferred his habitual expression to be a frown?

"She's got relatives there," Reece said. "Right?"

Maxey nodded. "An aunt and a cousin. Near Omaha. But I don't know . . . I don't think I really want to—"

"Sure you do." Reece broke open a package of crackers to crumble over his salad. "When was the last time you saw them?"

"My mother's funeral." She stabbed up a wedge of tomato. "Ten years ago."

"Ah, the Midwest in August," Clark said. "All that marvelous heat and humidity. A place where 'mean temperature' takes on a whole new significance."

"I like it hot," Maxey said.

"Sweet corn on the cob," Reece continued to talk it up. "Red-ripe tomatoes fresh off the vine."

"Shelly beans," she added. "Cabbage and new potatoes."

Clark pointed his knife into the air. "Mosquitoes, chiggers, poison ivy, tornadoes."

Maxey leaned forward, looking him in the eye. "Lightning bugs, dew, rivers with water in them, *trees.*"

"Maxey grew up in Ohio," Reece interceded. "Went to Ohio University."

"That so? What year did you graduate?"

"All I could afford was two semesters. Where'd you get your degrees?" She dragged out the last word, scoffing at his answer in advance.

"CU. CSU. Universities of Utah, Arizona, New Mexico, and Denver." He paused, looking down his nose at the dregs of his salad. "I finished maybe thirty credit hours." He looked up, smile in place.

Reece laughed. "A rolling stone gathers no diplomas."

Maxey wondered how long Clark would be content at the *Regard.* Maybe she could stand him for as long as that might be. Maybe a year from now she'd be begging him to stay and not sell his share to someone twice as undesirable.

Their steaks arrived, fragrant with garlic and steamy as the Midwest. Before tasting his, Clark shook on a layer of salt and pepper.

"Do you have relatives around here?" Maxey asked him, still thinking about his proclivity to roam.

He nodded, chewed, swallowed. "Ex-wife in Loveland. My mother's in a nursing home in Arvada. One grown son who lives in Cheyenne, but we don't communicate."

Now that the edge had worn off of her hunger, Maxey ate more deliberately, no longer begrudging the mushrooms that Reece kept forking onto his plate.

"Reece tells me—warned me—that you're a regular Nancy Drew," Clark said. "Solving murders right and left."

Maxey's dozing animosity snorted full awake. "Don't you guys patronize me. I didn't go looking for trouble, but I handled it competently when it arrived."

"You did, no question," Reece hastened to say. "No man could have done it better. If I'm ever knocked off, I hope you'll take the case."

"If you're ever knocked off, I'll probably be the one who did the knocking," Maxey grumbled.

"So are you going to solve any crimes in Nebraska?"

Clark's question was too dumb to deserve an answer. Ignoring him, she raised her empty tea glass at their waitress, who nodded on her way to another table, heaped plates balanced on her forearm. Maxey's eyes raked past Reece, then backtracked to his face, which was turned to stare at her.

"What?" she said.

"Is that why you're going there? To find out who killed your mom?"

"Oh, Reece, of course not. After all these years? How could— that's ridiculous."

"Sure," he said, drawing it out with lazy skepticism.

"No. I mean it. No."

The waitress arrived with the iced-tea pitcher, and she offered to bring the men coffee, fresh drinks, more water, dessert. While Reece and Clark were discussing and deciding, Maxey sipped tea and took cold, hard stock of what lay in the smallest cubbyholes of her mind.

Why should she spend two precious weeks visiting an elderly lady and a kid, people she didn't know very well and didn't want to know better? If she went to Nebraska—*if,* not *when*—the highlight would be a visit to her mother's grave, to make peace with the ghost of Peggy Witter Burnell.

2
. . .

American Airlines delivered Maxey to the Eppley Memorial Omaha Municipal Airport, and she picked up her rental Ford Escort with a minimum of waiting in line and paperwork.

She hoped the chilly drizzle that dulled the sky and gleamed on the asphalt parking lot was not an omen of the way her vacation was going to go. She swung her two pieces of scuffed black Samsonite into the trunk and tiptoed through puddles to the driver's door. The unfamiliar interior smelled like industrial-strength pine.

Taking time to find everything on the dash, she set the wipers on intermittent before tucking the automatic shift into drive and circling out of the lot.

She'd already set her watch forward an hour for the time zone, which made it 1:43 P.M. She should be in Gruder by 2:30, close to the ETA she'd quoted Janet two nights ago on the phone.

"Whee," Janet had squealed. "You really are going to visit us?"

"Yes, but don't go to any trouble. Don't clean the house or stock up the refrigerator."

"This is going to be so much fun. We can go to the Omaha art museum and the zoo and Boys Town and some of the state parks—"

"No, wait! Don't make big plans, okay? I just want to relax. Sleep and read. You know?"

"Absolutely. You can meet my book lovers' group. You wouldn't mind speaking to them about running a newspaper, would you? And you'll love my sewing club. Do you sew, Maxey?"

It was no use arguing long distance. Maxey would make a stand once she had taken possession of her aunt's guest bedroom.

She followed Route 165 to 75, went north on 75 to 91, west on 91 to 77, working her way up the highway steps toward Dodge County, home of Fremont Lakes, an ocean of corn, and Gruder, population 950, the last time anyone counted.

Traffic thinned as Omaha dropped behind her. The Escort's tires hissed on the wet pavement. There was no future in thinking of the past, but Maxey didn't have anything better to do.

She and her parents had probably driven this route many cornfields ago, on their way to visit Aunt Janet and Uncle Harold. The road trip from central Ohio, across three states, would have seemed endless to a preschooler, but she couldn't recall it at all now.

A semi, rattling empty, swept around the Escort and kicked oily water onto the windshield. Along the shoulder of the pavement, tattered blue cornflowers bobbed in the wake. When the wipers had smeared the windshield clear again, Maxey switched on the radio and surfed stations till she found one with an acceptable music-to-commercials ratio.

She didn't feel like thirty years old—however that felt. At thirty years old, her mother had a mere decade left to live. Her dad had died even younger, though no one would ever talk to Maxey about it, and she had no idea how or when or why. The implication had always been that Deon—Dee to his friends—Burnell had died as he had lived, unwisely and too well. Probably in one of the race cars he'd loved more than his wife and child.

Maxey didn't even know where he was buried.

Her mother was buried in the Gruder Grand View Cemetery. It had been on a day a lot like this one.

Maxey turned up the volume on Fleetwood Mac and wished she'd told Reece California instead of Nebraska.

■

The rain stopped falling, though the gray clouds still prowled like restless spirits.

Gruder hunkered in the flat farmland, an oasis of trees and roofs, dominated by a rocket-shaped water tower on spindly legs. Maxey wisely slowed for the railroad, up and over and bump, bump, bump. The grain elevator with its string of shiny storage bins looked deserted, useless this early in the season. A black dog strolled across the street in front of Maxey, confident he had the right of way in this, his territory.

She came to the center of town, marked by a four-way stop. After continuing straight on, she wondered if she should have turned. She didn't remember the flat-roofed cement-block Nazarene Church or the bright orange cottage with the WEE CARE DAY CARE sign out front. But then she found her landmark, a public park no bigger than a tennis court, crammed with a swing set, slide, sand pile, teeter-totter, jungle gym, three misshapen trees, and, at the moment, not one child.

Another half mile and the town gave up. The first farm southwest of the limits sign had been the Witter place since 1912. Great-Grandpa Arthur Witter built the house shortly before running off to Panama to help construct the canal. The men in Maxey's family were never known for constancy. How could she blame Reece for trying to carry on the tradition?

Winding the steering wheel a hard left into the gravel driveway, Maxey sized up the old homestead. The two-story clapboard house glimmered white between the gray sky and shaggy green lawn. Big trees—elms?—still overhung the roof, but they were riddled with dead limbs and rickety nests. The outbuildings, dominated by what had been a barn and now served as a garage, leaned out of true, but, like the house, they appeared to have been painted in recent memory.

The Escort bumped across the side yard. Maxey steered between a red Bronco and a rusted blue Mustang and shut off the engine. The wind gusted little yellow leaves against the windshield, and the damp pasted them there. Feeling watched and self-conscious, she opened the door and stepped into the cool swampy grass, yanking her purse out with her.

The back door—really a side door—stayed blank for maybe three seconds while Maxey waded toward it. Then there was a burst of motion as it flew open and Aunt Janet flew out. She waited at the top of the stone steps, arms outstretched and eager for the hugging to begin.

"I made it," Maxey said, climbing gamely toward her fate.

"Ooo, look at you," Janet exclaimed, encompassing her in an embrace that made any looking impossible. "All grown-up and gorgeous. I love your hair." She pushed Maxey away to study it. "Like a dish of yellow mashed potatoes."

Maxey doubted that anyone had ever told Princess Di that.

Janet's hair was more like cranberry sauce. At least the color was. It fell to her shoulders in luxuriant swirls that, given Janet's age and the fact that she'd previously had straight, fine, brown hair, didn't fool Maxey one bit. Still, one had to admire the old girl for striving to keep up appearances. She had on green eye shadow and a spicy perfume, too.

They stood on the porch—a slab of concrete with two wooden roof supports, it held one clay pot of bedraggled red geraniums and a braided rug that had been demoted to mud mat. The three kittens that were tumbling on the stone steps when Maxey arrived had scattered and hid before the invasion.

"Did you have a good trip?" Janet asked, one arm still strong around Maxey's shoulders. "Did they feed you on the plane? When did you leave Denver?"

Maxey opened her mouth to answer.

"Curtis! Get out here and welcome your cousin," Janet addressed the screen door.

Behind the age-blackened wire, a shadow shifted and loomed larger. "I'm coming," it said petulantly. The door squealed open and a gangling boy came through, staring resolutely at his bare feet.

"You remember my adopted son, Curtis," Janet said, impatiently waving him forward.

Maxey stuck her hand out to him before Janet could make them hug one another. "Sure. Hi, Curt."

His sweaty hand was big enough to have wrapped around hers twice. His grip was not too hard, not too soft, and brief as a blink. He glanced at Maxey before staring off across her shoulder toward the barn.

"You're what, a junior this year?" she asked.

"Senior." He rubbed the back of his neck. Taller than the women, he probably weighed less than either. Sandy hair standing on end, knobby knees showing through his ragged blue jeans, T-shirt broken out in random holes—a typical teen at home.

"Get Maxey's suitcases out of the car," Janet ordered.

Maxey offered Curtis the key. "Thanks. There are only two or I'd do it myself."

If Curtis recognized that this was a joke, he didn't let on. He ran down the steps as if he was escaping.

"Come on, come in," Janet said. "Gosh, it's good to have you here. You can have your mother's old room. I made a cherry pie. Do you still like cherry pie so well?"

While Janet prattled on, Maxey took in the sights and smells of the hard-used kitchen. The trestle table along one wall wore a yellow oilcloth and an untidy stack of newspapers and junk mail. White cupboards and counters made a U-turn around the rest of the walls. Apparently, Janet liked to have everything handy—the counters held more dishes and appliances than the cupboards' glass doors disclosed.

An owl-eyed cat, the same mottled orange and gray as the kittens, appeared in the dining room doorway, studied Maxey, and moved on about her business.

"Oh my, I almost got the crust too brown." Janet peeled a padded mitt off her hand and let the oven door clap shut.

The hot, red smell of cherries sent Maxey on an instant of flashback, to the cramped little kitchen in Ohio, its Frigidaire speckled with novelty magnets, the scrawny green plants lined up on the windowsill, the white gauze curtains hemmed with pink rickrack. It was in that kitchen, while she swung her legs under the table and spooned Cream of Wheat from a glass bowl inches below her chin, that her mother grimly announced that her daddy wasn't coming back.

The back door banged, jarring Maxey into the present, and Curtis shuffled into the room with her baggage. He paused and raised his eyebrows at his mother.

"In the southeast bedroom, Curtis. You know that. Now, Maxey, if I've forgotten anything you need, you just let me know." Janet cupped her hands to test-pat the curls around her face.

She did look well preserved for sixty-some years. Square shoulders, a trim waist, only a hint of tummy. Her upper arms, exposed by a sleeveless denim dress, wobbled with very minor dewlaps. Her white legs bared the faintest of blue veins and one yellow bruise at coffee-table height.

Curtis came clattering down the back stairs and hung from the door frame before jittering to a parade rest beside the table.

"Maxey, you want a piece of pie now?" Janet asked.

She didn't, but Curtis was nodding and rubbing his hands. The airline's peanuts and apple juice hadn't stuck to her ribs, anyway.

"A little piece for me and a big piece for Curtis, please. First, I have to wash up."

"You know where it is." Janet began rummaging plates out of the counter stock. She waved impatiently in front of her face. "Curtis, when are you going to fix the front-door screen like I told you? The flies are driving me nuts."

His mumbled answer included something about staples.

The back stairs, narrow and steep, came out right beside the southeast bedroom. Passing the open door, Maxey saw that Curtis had rucked up the white chenille bedspread with her two cases. Otherwise, the room was neat as a very small pin. It contained one oak bedside stand that matched the bookcase-headboarded bed, one red-and-pink rag rug, one bureau with a wavy mirror, one walk-in closet (if you didn't want to walk far), one white-curtained window on each outside wall, and a washed-out print of a sailboat on a lake.

Maxey continued down the creaky hardwood hall to the bathroom, shoved open the door, and teetered on the threshold, all of her attention irresistibly drawn to the pale bare buttocks of the man standing in front of the commode.

He looked back at her over his shoulder. "Well, drat."

Belatedly, she shucked off her surprised fascination and backed out. "Excuse me. I didn't know—"

"Well, of course you didn't. My fault." Maxey slammed the door and the stranger raised his voice through it. "I snuck up the front stairs, thinking I'd get presentable. Hee, hee, what a view I did present. I'll be out in a minute."

Not wanting to appear overeager about that, Maxey slipped back down the hall to her bedroom and eased the door shut. She busied herself hanging clothes in the closet, speculating about the man's identity.

The Witter place began as a farm. The acreage had diminished over the years, sold to bankroll college educations or new automobiles or, during the Depression, groceries. Maxey had an idea that what little land remained was worked by a sharecropper from a neighboring farm.

Maybe that farmer was Mr. Dimple Cheeks.

She straightened convulsively as a smart rap sounded on her door. "It's all yours," the stranger called before he clattered down the stairs.

Maxey followed him a few minutes later, dreading the embarrassment of their next meeting. She could hear him talking in the kitchen, something about Chubby Pitkin's posthole digger, which seemed to confirm her guess as to his role here.

"Oh, here she is." Janet welcomed Maxey as if she'd been gone for hours. "Maxey, I want you to meet Scotty."

The old man didn't look as old as she'd been led to believe by her first, admittedly one-sided view of him. Maxey guessed he hadn't been getting senior discounts for more than a year or two. Red-orange hair bristled on his head, gray whiskers sprouted from his cheeks, and his blue sweatpants clashed with his turquoise muscle shirt. He grinned, exposing a disarming Alfred E. Neuman gap in his upper front teeth.

"Scotty Springer. Delighted to meet you face-to-face," he said to Maxey, and one eyelid slipped to half-mast. "Janet has told me so much about you, her favorite niece. Excuse me for staring—just trying to see your halo."

Maxey laughed. "I'm her favorite niece because I'm her only niece."

Janet dealt out three pieces of pie à la mode and three steaming coffee mugs on one end of the tabletop. "Okay, sit down and dig in."

Maxey dragged out the chair across the table from Scotty, leaving the end place between them for Janet.

"Has Curtis had his?" Maxey asked, not wanting him to miss out, since it was his fault she was eating this hot and cold tender perfection now.

"Bolted down two slices and a quart of milk. And he'll be hungry in an hour," Janet observed with pride. "Now then, Maxey, I want to explain the situation to you. I'm sure you're shocked that your auntie has taken a lover and is living in sin, with no intention of doing the right thing."

The tops of Scotty's ears turned hot pink. He watched his pie as if someone might steal it.

Maxey didn't know why her aunt felt the need to explain something this personal to a niece she scarcely knew. But that was Janet. She talked openly about everything important to her. Introducing Curtis as her adopted son, for example. Who the hell cared that he was adopted? Except Curtis, maybe. It was just Janet's way. Put her with a stranger at a bus stop and she'd confide how she planned to vote in the next election, how much money she had in the bank, and why she was on her way to the gynecologist.

"Janet, you don't need to explain anything. It's none of my business, and anyway, I sure couldn't be first in line to cast any stones."

"No, no, it isn't right, but it's the way it is. After your uncle Harold died, I was alone for fifteen years." She forked up a big bite and held it at the ready. "Yep. I've tried alone, and I've tried Scotty, and Scotty's better."

Now Scotty's whole ears glowed rosy.

"I'm glad you have each other," Maxey said. "I'm still searching for the right someone to sin with."

"It's all the government's doing. The minute we get married, our income taxes go up and our Social Security benefits go down. I'd lose Harold's lodge pension, which isn't all that much, but it's more than nothing."

" 'I have enough money to last me the rest of my life, if I don't buy anything,' " Scotty said, and he seemed pleased at the laugh

Maxey gave him. "I think it was Jackie Mason said that," he admitted.

Janet didn't laugh. Eyebrows at a pained slant, she pressed on. "We've got friends in the same situation. It isn't right, the U.S. government pimping us seniors."

"I never realized. Or I guess I did, but I never thought—" Maxey held up a forefinger. "I'll write an editorial for the *Regard*."

Janet sat back, her hand spread on her chest. "You won't use our names."

"No, of course not." Maxey sipped at her coffee. She grinned at Scotty. "I'll say, 'Maxey Burnell's aunt in Nebraska.' "

"Oh, sure, make light of me. But I tell you, it gets harder to laugh every day," Janet said. "I had to move Scotty in here with me. Had to. For protection."

"From what?"

"Men! Calling on the phone or knocking on the door, all hours of the day and night. Thinking because I was a widow, I must be a., rich, and b., horny as an armadillo."

Maxey snickered into her coffee cup. "So how long have you two known each other? Where'd you meet?"

Scotty spoke up. "On the swings, on the playground behind the elementary school."

"About sixty years ago," Janet clarified.

"Ah." Maxey nodded her understanding. "Childhood sweethearts."

"No way. He was a snot-nosed little show-off. Couldn't stand him. He moved to Omaha in seventh grade and nobody missed him."

"Janet," Maxey protested.

"She's right," Scotty said. "But then she was a prissy little tattletale, and I didn't miss her, either."

Janet stood up to get the coffeepot. "He came back to Gruder to retire three years ago. First thing he did was ask if pretty little Janet Witter was still around."

Scotty put his hand over his cup. "No more for me. Actually"—he leaned forward to confide in Maxey—"she cornered me in the post office and hung on my pant leg till I promised to come to supper."

"You old coot," Janet said without malice.

"Well," he said, pushing away from the table, "I guess I'll go wheedle a posthole digger out of a friend."

"Putting up a fence?" Maxey scraped up the last bit of pie.

"Jannie wants one of those newfangled ecological things—what do you call 'em? Outdoor clothesline." He whisked a billed cap from a coatrack by the door and hustled outside.

"So, honey, what do you want to do first?" Janet asked, rinsing dishes at the sink.

Maxey twisted around in her chair, squinting at her aunt's silhouette against the white sky through the window. "I don't want you to entertain me."

"Pooh. It's no trouble. How often do I get the chance?" Janet strode to the table and searched through the pile of newspapers. "I gave Scotty a membership to triple A last Christmas. We never go anywhere, but he likes geography. He reads these like they were regular books." She held aloft a *North Central TourBook*. A road map fell out of it. "Here, you can use this while you're here."

"Thanks, I will. Janet, sometime while I'm here, I'd like to talk to you about my mother."

"Sure. You want to see where she went to school? See where we lived when she was a kid? I'll bet the Darnells would let us walk through the house. I'd like to see it again myself."

"Well, maybe. What I'd really like to do is know more about her life right before she died. We didn't see each other much for that last year or so, I'm ashamed to say. I don't feel her death as a closure. You know what I mean?"

"I guess," Janet said doubtfully.

Maxey sighed. "When she died, I was too young and too—flighty,

I guess—even to read all the news accounts. We weren't close, Mom and I, and I was distracted by trying to pass spring exams at the university, worried about how I was going to get enough money for next fall's tuition. God. Selfish? I'm sweating a few stupid classes, and she's gone forever. I didn't mourn her properly then. I want to do it now."

"That's fine. You mourn all you want, nothing wrong with that. Go out to the cemetery and have yourself a good cry." Janet patted at her dress pocket, withdrew a tissue, and dabbed at her mouth with it. Her hands trembled.

"I'm not very good at crying," Maxey said. "What I'd like to do is get the facts that I didn't want to deal with at the time. I'm not even clear on where it happened." Maxey's face felt stiff, and it hurt to smile. "Of course, what I'd really like to know is who killed her."

Janet sat down hard in the nearest kitchen chair. "No. No you don't. Peggy wouldn't want you nosing around in what's over and done."

Maxey gave a rueful wag of her head. "It wouldn't be the first time I disappointed her."

"You don't understand what you're asking for. You have no idea in the world what you're getting into."

Her aunt's blank white face shamed Maxey into a sweep of guilt. She stretched awkwardly across the table to pat Janet's shoulder. "I didn't mean to upset you. I should have known you'd rather not talk about it. I can ask someone else to—"

"No! There's no one knows better than I do. I'll tell you exactly what happened, even though you're going to regret you made me."

Frowning, Maxey withdrew to her own side of the table. The room suddenly dimmed and a gust of new rain splattered against the house.

"There's no use your hunting for the murderer of your mother, Maxey, because I know who did it. I saw him."

This was the last thing and the best thing that Maxey could have expected. "You saw him? Would you know him if you saw him again?"

Janet laughed one short, ugly note that had nothing to do with humor. "I guess I would. I guess I did. It was your father."

3

. . .

"You know as well as I do, my father's dead," Maxey said. "He died when I was a kid. You must have seen someone who looked like him."

Janet shook her head and reached out to touch Maxey's hand, fisted on the table. The hand rolled over of its own accord and gripped Janet's.

"Honey, right this minute, your father is living it up, probably with some woman, free as tumbleweed."

Maxey felt her own face draining as white as Janet's. "Alive? Why didn't you tell me? Why did everyone say he was dead?"

"Well, that's what women do tell their children when old daddy deserts them. Better to think he's dead than to think he doesn't love the family enough to stick around. Right? For all practical purposes, Deon Burnell had sure enough passed away."

Janet flexed her fingers, and Maxey realized she'd been squeezing them for dear life. Letting go, she rubbed her forehead.

She was a daughter again. The idea wouldn't lie still and let her examine it.

"Now, Maxey, I know you. I can just bet you've already begun planning how to get in touch with him. Just forget that. Forget him. If that man wanted anything to do with you, don't you think he'd have looked you up before now?"

The words, which should have hurt, rolled off Maxey like the raindrops skidding down the windows. "He didn't know where I was."

"I knew where you were. All he had to do was pick up the phone and give me a call."

"But he knew how you felt about him, Janet. He must have thought you wouldn't tell him—"

"Damn right I wouldn't. I'd have slammed down that phone so fast, it'd have made his ears ring."

"See? Okay, so where was he the last time you heard anything of him?"

Janet slapped the tabletop with the flat of her hand. "He was in this house, shooting your mother. For a reporter, you surely do a poor job of listening."

"You saw him with the gun in his hand? Saw him pull the trigger?"

"No." Janet sighed. "But I did see him drive away. And when I came inside, there she lay. So bloody and so . . . gone." She jumped up to rip a fresh tissue from a box on top of the refrigerator and blew her nose.

Maxey stood, too, and reached for a tissue for herself. "All right. I want to hear the entire story, beginning to end—all the details that I never bothered to get before. Like, exactly where did it happen?"

"I'll tell you the entire story one time, but then I don't want to discuss it anymore. Not now, not ever."

"No, Aunt Janet. I can't promise that."

Janet set her knuckles on her hips and glared at Maxey. Maxey mimicked the pose and pretended to glare back.

"Oh, all right, damn it anyway. Come in here." Janet led off through the dining room.

Maxey remembered the big round claw-footed table hogging the center of the floor. It had been festive, one long-gone holiday—a pink tablecloth, heavy-handled silverware, a fat red candle in the midst of evergreen sprigs. Now the table held four stacks of folded laundry, a wooden bowl of bruised peaches, a pair of black binoculars, a portable radio shaped like a guitar, and perhaps ten years' worth of *National Geographic* magazines.

Except for eight curve-backed, bowlegged chairs pushed against the walls, the rest of the room was empty. Their footsteps echoed on the bare oak floor.

"Why was Mom here when she died? We—she—still lived in the house in Ohio."

"Just visiting for the summer. You know she'd been laid off at the box factory. Jobs weren't plentiful right then right there, and she'd about decided to move back to Gruder. That would have been so nice, having her for company in this big old house." Janet stopped in the living room archway and shook one pointing finger. "We found her over there on the floor, by the doors to the front hall. Except the doors were open then."

The square living room was as crowded with furniture as the dining room was empty. Fat overstuffed chairs and one lumpy sofa formed a semicircle around the TV set, which sat in front of the black-screened, gray-tiled fireplace. In the front bay window, a white wooden stepladder had been converted into a plant stand, every step holding or hanging more than one pot. Assorted tables and chests bore assorted knickknacks, vases, lamps. In one corner sat a treadle sewing machine; in another, a forties radio. The cabbage rose wallpaper had faded to cauliflower. The Oriental carpet was worn down to an Oriental sheet blanket.

Everything looked as shabby and clean as a newly opened flea market.

Maxey crossed the creaking floor to the hall doors and folded one open. On her left, the glass and wood front door stood ajar, its screen door letting in the green smell of rain. To her right, the open staircase marched up to a landing, hung a military right turn, and disappeared behind an upstairs wall.

"Here?" Maxey said, studying the oak planks underfoot, half-afraid of finding bloodstains.

"Yes."

"Facing which way?"

"Same as you. Toward the living room."

"And which direction did the shot come from?"

Janet backed up a few steps, to the center of the living room. She spread her arms. "About here."

Through the screen door, Maxey could see a slice of the big stone porch, an expanse of unkempt lawn, and a straight stretch of east-west road. She ducked her head to squint out the living room windows flanking the fireplace. They overlooked the driveway.

"Where were you when you thought you saw Dad?"

"There's no use you assuming I made a mistake, Maxey Diane. I heard the shot, ran around the southwest corner of the house, and saw Deon come flying out the kitchen door. He leapt into his black Chevy pickup and drove away. You can still see the low spots in the drive where his tires churned up gravel."

Maxey sat on the second step of the stairway and hugged her knees. Janet joined her, grunting as she settled down, putting one comforting arm across Maxey's back.

"The boys and I were picking strawberries in the garden out back. Curtis and his friend Lance Chalmers. Peggy had a headache that day, and she'd gone upstairs to take a nap after lunch. Now it was about three o'clock, and we'd just about covered the berry patch. But we ran out of baskets, so I was on my way to the house to get a few more."

Maxey imagined she could smell the warm, sweet strawberries, but it was probably only cherry pie.

"I'd gotten to the end of the row, ready to set foot in the grass of the backyard, and there was this sharp *crack,* and the boys looked at me and I looked at them, and we all knew what it was. I mean, you don't grow up in the country with menfolk who like to hunt and not learn the sound of a rifle."

Maxey nodded.

"Well, I didn't have the first idea why we'd heard it, but I knew what we'd heard, so I started running, like I said, around the corner of the house, and there was Deon. Like I said."

"But if you told the sheriff, why didn't he—"

"Hearsay." Janet's outrage roughened her voice. "The boys didn't see him, so it was my word against Deon's. He had an alibi. Politics is what it really was. Dee had friends in high places."

"What was his alibi?"

"I forget. He supposedly wasn't in the county. I didn't pay much attention to his story. I knew what I'd seen, and no alibi on earth could shake my conviction that my baby sister was murdered by her no-account estranged husband."

Maxey gritted her teeth against an angry protest. This was her father, after all, and innocent till Maxey should find proof otherwise. But arguing with Janet wouldn't do anyone any good.

"What was his motive, Janet?"

"How should I know?"

"What do you think was his motive? You must have thought about it."

"No. I didn't want to think about it. Husbands and wives always have plenty of things to kill each other over. Men and women do, whether they're married or not. Many's the time I could have strangled Scotty. And Harold, oh my, yes." She hugged Maxey closer. "I know this is hard for you, sweetheart. It's a shock, finding out your dad's alive and a killer. The quicker you accept it, resign yourself to it, the sooner you can go back to living your own life."

"I can't accept it until I check it all out for myself." Maxey wiped both cheeks hard with the heels of her hands. "I have to find him."

Janet sighed and pulled her arm away, leaning into the far banister. "Stubborn. You got that from your grandpa Witter."

Maxey leaned against her own banister and patted Janet's knee. "And speaking of Grandpa, it was his rifle, right?"

"Yes. Nasty thing. As soon as the sheriff allowed, I got rid of it. Took it to a gun dealer in Omaha."

"No fingerprints on it?"

"Course not. Wiped clean as a Sprat platter."

A blue-black fly blundered around the walls, shooting landings on the furniture without ever stopping.

"Did she—was death instantaneous?" Maxey asked.

"You know it was. Shot through the head, above her left eye. Surely you knew that much."

"Yes. I just want to make certain I have everything straight, all the facts."

"The only fact that you need is—"

"I know, I know. Maybe my dad wasn't the only person here. Maybe he was a witness."

"Uh-huh, and how did this alleged other person escape the notice of me and the two boys? The three of us reached the living room maybe half a minute after the shot. We'd have seen anyone heading toward the road. The only someone I saw was Deon."

Maxey stood and paced aimlessly into the living room. "I must have read a few newspaper accounts. Why didn't any of them mention him? He wasn't listed as a survivor in her obituary. Why didn't he come to the funeral?"

Deliberately, Janet jutted her chin to blow upward at her humid bangs. "What good would any of that done? Peggy was better off without him, in death as in life."

The rain hesitated and stopped, leaving the eaves gurgling. A fast-moving station wagon swished by on the road.

Maxey glanced around the room; it bided, dim and serene. "I have to talk to him."

■

"Spaghetti? Yum."

Janet had been terse and preoccupied the rest of the afternoon. Feeling guilty for making her aunt unhappy, Maxey worked up a convincing enthusiasm for the evening's entertainment—a spaghetti supper at the Christian Church.

"Do I need to change clothes?" she asked, looking down at her chino slacks, brushing lint off the front of her moss green silk shirt.

"There'll be worse there," Janet answered ambiguously.

Scotty's muddy red Bronco muttered and squeaked past the kitchen window. In a few moments, he stamped onto the porch. Whistling into the kitchen, he brought along the scent of sweat and liquor.

"Ladies," he greeted them, spinning his Farm Bureau billed cap onto its hook. He whistled another few vague notes and wiggled his eyebrows at Maxey, who sat at the kitchen table with a cold cup of coffee and the Nebraska map.

Scotty wiped his mouth with the back of his hand. " 'I know only two tunes. One of them is "Yankee Doodle," and the other isn't.' " Rewarded by Maxey's chuckle, he added, "Ulysses S. Grant said that."

"Did you get the posthole digger?" Janet asked, her tone implying that she knew he'd failed.

"What's your hurry? You can't dry clothes in the rain. I'll get the job done, Jannie." He grinned at Maxey. " 'Work is the refuge of people who have nothing better to do.' Oscar Wilde wrote that."

"You've got about twenty minutes to get presentable for the church supper," Janet said from beside the sink, where she was filling a watering can for a fifth trip to the living room plant ladder.

"Tell Curtis when you go upstairs. We have to leave in about twenty minutes."

Maxey smiled up at the old man. The borrowed map crackled under her elbows as she leaned to locate Dodge County.

"Where's the sheriff's office for this area?" she asked softly as soon as Janet crossed into the dining room.

"Fremont. Why? You going to turn yourself in?"

Laughing, Maxey shook her head, trying to think of a snappy comeback, but Scotty charged up the back stairs, too fast for her.

Forty minutes later, the four of them trooped into the sharp-steepled redbrick church on the south boundary of Gruder. It smelled of oregano and garlic.

Maxey glimpsed the sanctuary, dim as a theater, the wooden benches planted in rows down to the fenced-in altar. Then she was guided down the bare wood steps to the basement, where long tables draped in white paper waited to be despoiled by splattered spaghetti sauce and coffee rings.

Four women and one man hovered behind the serving table at the far end. One of the ladies, wearing a Ruth Buzzi hair net and a white butcher's apron, looked up at their approach and waved extravagantly, as if she was flagging a bus.

Janet waved back. "Get out your money, Scotty. What's two-fifty times four?"

"Let me buy," Maxey said, pawing through her shoulder bag for a twenty. "It's the cheapest meal I'll get a chance to treat."

They stopped at the end of the serving table, where an elderly man with sparse hair and even sparser teeth cheerfully counted Maxey's change from a gray metal box. "Okay, you've paid your toll, folks. You can move on."

Maxey motioned Curtis to go first, and he swaggered self-consciously forward to accept a salad plate and two chunks of garlic bread from a heavyset woman who wheezed when she breathed.

Maxey, Scotty, and Janet did a three-part do-si-do of politeness before Janet stepped in behind Curtis and Maxey followed her.

"Nice rain we had," Scotty said to the next customers to arrive.

"Ready to see the sun," a woman answered.

"Well, like George Carlin says, the weather forecast for tonight is dark."

Maxey laughed, but the people to whom Scotty addressed the remark didn't seem to get it.

"Meat or vegetarian?" A perspiring lady in a fuchsia-flowered apron over a red-flowered dress smiled at Maxey, serving spoon poised.

"Vegetarian, please and thank you."

The spoon swooped into the stainless-steel pan on her right and brought up a steaming red portion of sauce to spread on a generous nest of pale spaghetti. Meanwhile, the server was saying, "I bet you're Janet's niece from Boulder, Colorado. They got a lot of vegetarians there, I hear."

"Yeah, we're pretty weird all right." Maxey grinned.

"Uh-oh. Are you a vegetarian?" Scotty asked. "Jannie's been stockpiling chicken and roasts and hamburger to feed an army of nieces."

"I'm a lapsed vegan," she admitted. "I'm trying to form a Meat Eaters Anonymous."

The little line had ground to a halt, the traffic jam caused by Janet's pausing to converse with the hair-netted friend, who was dispensing beverages. "But what do doctors know? They're human beings, like the rest of us."

"Oh, Inez, you better not wait too long to do something about it."

"Well, a second opinion wouldn't hurt. Do you know anything about a Dr. Avillez over in Schuyler?"

"Come on," Scotty said to Maxey. "I'll sneak back for our drinks later." He led her to a table and held a folding chair for her in an awkward, old-fashioned show of chivalry.

Curtis had found a friend at another table. The two young men hunched over their plates, eating and talking, their backs to the rest of the room. While Maxey watched, Curtis elbowed his friend in the ribs, the friend fended him off with a forearm to the chin, and the two embarked on an adolescent scuffle for possession of a salt shaker.

Maxey leaned sideways toward Scotty. "Is that Lance Chalmers by any chance?"

"Sure enough. Real nice kid. You know him?"

"No." Maxey twirled pasta around her fork.

"That's his mama, jawing with Janet."

"Oh, uh-huh." The sauce tasted homemade, rich and tangy. She hoped seconds were allowed.

"Nice lady." He lowered his head beside Maxey's shoulder to murmur, "Cancer. Always fighting cancer."

"Oh, that's too bad."

Maxey cast a quick look over her shoulder. Inez Chalmers was drawing a cup of coffee for a farmer who looked as if he'd come straight from the fields, denim overalls, muddy boots, and all. Take away the hair net and Inez could be called attractive. Plump, matronly, but attractive.

"Is there a Mr. Chalmers?" Maxey asked.

Scotty sat back and craned to look around the growing crowd. "He's probably here somewhere."

"Nice guy?"

"Far as I know. But then, 'I never met—' "

" 'A man I didn't like,' " Maxey said with him and laughed. "Will Rogers said that."

"Or was it Mae West?"

They were both giggling when Janet drew out the chair next to Maxey's. "What's the joke?" Before either could answer, she was waving and calling to another friend who'd just walked down the stairs.

"All the quotations you can spiel off, you must be a marathon reader, Scotty. And then"—Maxey chewed and swallowed—"you remember it all."

He shrugged. "I was born to read. My last words will be, 'Soon as I finish this page.' "

Maxey chuckled. "Who said that?"

Scotty craned to look over his left shoulder and then his right. "Didn't I?" He caught sight of someone at a middle table and waved. A florid-faced man with bushy gray hair and shoulders like a retired wrestler lifted a palm in acknowledgement. "That's Richard Chalmers, there."

Maxey smiled when Chalmers looked at her, and he nodded as if he knew her. He undoubtedly knew who she was. Janet would have briefed the entire population of Gruder that her only niece was poised to visit.

Scotty scraped back his chair. "Black coffee, right?"

"Please."

"Need anything, Jannie?"

Janet shook her head, mouth too full to speak.

The room had steadily filled with hungry church supporters. A goodly proportion of the town's population, surely even some people who normally attended the concrete-block Nazarene Church near its center, were eating spaghetti tonight. Across the table from Maxey, a family of six, the children as blond as their father and petite as their mother, sat shoulder-to-shoulder like birds on a wire, eating and twittering.

Someone kicked the back leg of Maxey's chair. She glanced around, to find Curtis bending to speak to Janet. Behind him, Lance Chalmers fidgeted with a set of keys, jiggling them from hand to hand. Maxey smiled at him, but he didn't notice, or didn't feel like smiling. He was a good-looking kid—tanned, blue-eyed, square-jawed, with brown hair long enough to be twirled around some lucky girl's finger.

"I'm going to spend the night at Lance's. Okay?" Curtis said, smoothing his mother's rumpled collar in a nervous, protective gesture.

Janet nodded, patting at his withdrawing hand, and leaned to continue a conversation with the neighbor on her right, a wispy white-haired lady with a laugh like Phyllis Diller's.

Maxey twisted in her chair. "Hi, Lance. I'm Curtis's cousin, Maxey."

"Yeah, I know." He shuffled away, Curtis in tow.

Feeling vaguely insulted—the prodigal daughter rebuffed—Maxey turned back to her dinner.

"The new generation has no patience for small talk," Scotty said. "It's TV. It conditions kids to have attention spans the width and depth of spot commercials."

The boys trotted up the basement steps, loose-limbed and exuberant, youth on the brink of adulthood. Maxey wouldn't have returned to that carefree, insecure age for all the allowance money in the world.

The little family across the table finished eating and fluttered away. Maxey pushed aside her empty dishes, wishing for another round of pasta. No one else had gone back for seconds. She told herself a sour-grapes tale of how she'd weigh less in the morning for having practiced restraint tonight.

"Hello, folks," Richard Chalmers said, drawing out a chair across from Scotty and sitting. He leaned back, crossed his arms on his abundant chest, and studied Maxey. "You look like your mama."

She hadn't expected anyone to mention her mother voluntarily. It flustered her for a moment. "Think so? And Lance looks like you."

"In the face, maybe. He doesn't have my bulldog build. He's more a rottweiler." He pounded the table in front of Scotty. "Right, McSpringer? Good supper, huh?"

Scotty dug a toothpick out of his breast pocket and began to probe with it. "Fit for a Pope."

"Richard, I want you to see that Inez doesn't procrastinate about that lump," Janet said, bossy as a schoolteacher. "You take her over to Schuyler the first of the week."

"I'll do that. Don't you worry." Distracted by a longhaired woman who squeezed his shoulder as she passed behind him, Richard grabbed at her hand, missed, and smiled after her.

Scotty leaned to look around Maxey at Janet. "Ready to go?"

"I'm working on half a cup of coffee yet." She slurped at it to show good faith.

Inez Chalmers came up to the group, folding her apron. "I've done my share. Let's go home, Richard."

"Okay, Mrs. C." Richard stood and hauled up his pants by the belt. The buckle involved a lot of silver and inlaid turquoise. "Maybe I can catch the end of the Cardinals game."

Janet thumped down her empty cup to signal she was ready to leave also. It took the party of five a minute or two to reach the stairs, as Janet and Inez paused every few feet to speak to someone.

"How long you going to be in Gruder, Maxey?" Inez asked as they finally crowded out the front door.

Before Maxey could answer, Janet spoke up. "As long as it takes her to track down Peggy's killer."

The Chalmerses came to a hard stop on the church porch, and everyone else bumped into someone.

"Oh dear," Inez said, turning liquid eyes to study Maxey in the light from an overhead spotlight. "You don't want to do that."

"Aunt Janet is exaggerating. Although I would like to see Mom's murder solved—for my own peace of mind."

Richard jabbed several fingers into his shirt pocket and hauled out a crumpled package of cigarettes. Shaking one free, he stowed the pack again and patted pockets for a light. "You start snooping around, you're liable to run into some real trouble. You want to get yourself killed, too? Course"—he laughed, a barking, coughing sound—"I guess dead is the ultimate peace of mind."

"Hush," his wife said, taking his arm to pull him down the shallow steps into the parking area. "You don't want to scare her."

"The hell I don't. Murder isn't all neat and civilized like on TV, like Jennifer Fletcher or whoever. It's smelly and ugly and disgusting. It's not Miss Marple, it's—" He waved his arms, searching for the example. "—John Wayne Gacy and Speck and Jack the Ripper."

"Maxey knows that, I'm sure. She's a newspaper woman," Inez said, giving Richard a shove in the back to get him walking again.

Maxey thought Janet smiled before she turned into the shadows. Apparently, she was enjoying Richard's reaction to her overdramatic and not entirely accurate announcement.

"I'm really only here for a couple of weeks," Maxey called after the Chalmerses. "And I'm as interested in finding my father as I am in finding the person who murdered my mother."

"Now that's a redundant statement if I ever heard one," Janet muttered, following Scotty to the Bronco.

Inez and Richard moved farther down the line of cars to their pickup truck, he still expounding about the unsavoriness of murder and she still prodding him to shut up and walk.

Maxey waited for Scotty to unlock her door. The vehemence of Richard Chalmers's disapproval seemed excessive. She felt herself filing his reaction away for future reference and knew she was hooked, knew she'd shifted from tourist to investigative reporter.

Maxey crawled into the back of the Bronco and leaned her head against the cool window. "I think I'm coming down with jet lag."

Scotty started the engine, tripped the lights, and watched in the rearview mirror as the truck roared to life and beat him backing out. Richard must have remembered he was in a hurry to get home to watch baseball. As the dark pickup passed behind them, it tooted two notes—"good" and "bye."

The Bronco swung out and pointed homeward.

"Is there anyone in Boulder you want to phone to tell them you arrived safely?" Janet sounded tired herself.

"No thanks. If I hadn't arrived safely, they'd have heard about it."

"Do you have someone special?" Janet tipped her head against the backrest. "What should I call him? *Boyfriend* is too adolescent; *lover* is too lascivious; *significant other* is too coy."

"How about *lucky sucker?*" Scotty suggested.

"I've been dating a very nice fireman. His name's Calen Taylor."

Janet sniffed. " 'Very nice,' huh? That tells me right there it isn't serious."

"We've only known each other a year."

"You only knew Reece for six months, as I recall, before that relationship got hot and heavy."

Maxey squirmed. "How'd we get onto this subject, anyhow?"

"No, it's okay that you're moving slower this time. It's only natural, once you've been burned. But see, I have a legitimate reason to be nosy. I wanted to know if it was okay to introduce you to some of the local eligibles, invite a few possibles to dinner while you're here."

"No matchmaking, Janet. For one thing, I'll make my own matches. And for another, I don't want to find some great guy here in Nebraska, when I live and work in Colorado."

Scotty braked for a small animal crossing the road. Red reflector eyes glowed and were gone.

"Oh, all right. You're just no fun at all, Maxey Diane. You're too much like your mother."

A memory of Peggy's face flashed through Maxey's mind. It wasn't smiling. It wasn't happy. It wasn't even contented. It occurred to Maxey that her mother had always looked like a murder about to happen.

4

Of course, once Maxey was washed and nightied and tucked into her too-soft bed, she wasn't sleepy anymore. After five minutes of rumpling the bedclothes, she got up and turned on the ceiling fixture. The only light in the room, it shone too brightly on the foot of the bed and not brightly enough everywhere else.

Maxey sat against the headboard and opened her notebook to two blank pages. At the top of one, she wrote "Dad," and at the top of the other, "Mom." Under each heading, she numbered from one to an optimistic ten. Then she doodled in the margins for a while, boxes inside boxes, as she tried to think how to get a lead on her dad's whereabouts.

He'd run away from home to be a race-car driver. She wrote "Race cars" after number one. Then she doodled some more.

Turning to the "Mom" list, she wrote "Sheriff." No one else could give her more accurate, unemotional information about Peggy's death. That list gradually grew.

1. Sheriff (interview).
2. Find out. Who were her friends?
3. Who were her enemies!
4. What did she do that morning?
5. Whom did she see the week before she died?
6. What kind of mood was she in just b.s.d.?
7. Talk to Richard Chalmers, maybe find out why he was so uptight tonight.
8. Should I bother Curtis and Lance on this—try to get what they remember? Pretty traumatic stuff for little kids.
9. Interview any witnesses whose names come up when—see 1 above.
10. The rifle.

She yawned hugely and lost her train of thought, then grimaced at the almost blank page for "Dad." Deon was her first priority, but how could she find him when she didn't know where to begin?

Maybe if she focused on her mother's death, someone would give her a clue to her father's life.

She yawned again and slid lower into the bed. What had she been going to write about the rifle? Shutting her eyes, the better to think, she didn't open them again until sunlight diluted the artificial light, making her feel guilty for the wasted electricity. She lifted the notebook off her chest and read through what she'd written.

What was it that bothered her about the rifle?

The scents of coffee and bacon and maple syrup undulated up the back stairs and gave her something more pleasant to think about.

■

Maxey and Janet lingered over breakfast together. Scotty had bolted his and ridden out in the Bronco to round up a posthole digger.

"This morning, I'm hosting a meeting of the Gruder Timely Stitchers," Janet said around a forkful of scrambled eggs. "All the ladies will be excited to meet you."

"They'd be really disappointed once we got past the introductions. I don't know basting from batting. I mend my clothes with safety pins and adhesive tape."

"You wouldn't be expected to sew," Janet sneered. "You'd be expected to admire everyone else's sewing, and answer questions about the newspaper business and your love life."

Maxey fortified herself with a swallow of coffee. "I'm sorry, Janet, but there's something I need to do this morning instead."

"Oh." Janet's lower lip puckered out and down. "I wanted to show you off."

"Maybe I'll be back early. I'll try to be—in time to sign autographs and offer my ring to be kissed."

Janet sniffed. "You have that kind of attitude, I'm just as glad you won't be around."

"They'll like your version of me a lot more than the real me," Maxey agreed.

"So what's your important errand?"

Maxey swallowed more coffee, reluctant to spoil Janet's breakfast with the answer. "I'm going over to Fremont and uh . . . just sort of talk to the sheriff. About—you know."

Janet threw down her fork and pushed back her chair.

"I thought maybe he could help me get a lead on where to find Deon," Maxey rushed to add.

"After ten years? Not likely." Janet stood up and collected her dishes. "I thought we were going to have such fun together, and now . . . well, shoot."

The sink rang with the silverware she threw into it.

Maxey sat up straighter, realizing what she'd wanted to know about the rifle. "How did it get in the living room?"

"How did what get in the living room?" Janet grumbled.

"Grandpa's rifle. Where did you keep it?"

The floor creaked as Janet crossed to the table for another load of dishes. "In the junk room." She pinched her lips together and returned to the sink.

"Which room is that?"

"The little bedroom."

"Upstairs? Across from the bathroom?"

Janet nodded.

"Then how did it get down to the living room to shoot Mom?"

Janet shrugged. "Sheriff Zanetta speculated she brought it downstairs herself for some reason. He said she must have carried it with her for protection. Heard a stranger in the house." Janet deliberately turned to show Maxey a meaningful look. "Or not a stranger, I say."

"Janet." Maxey gave her an equally meaningful look. "That's exactly why I have to talk to the sheriff. I'm going to show you that you're wrong about my dad."

■

So now it was midmorning, and she'd found the stone justice building that housed the sheriff's office near the center of Fremont, and she'd gotten as far as the receptionist's counter, which divided the uniforms from the civilians.

"I'd like to speak to Sheriff Zanetta," Maxey said.

The female officer's short gray hair stood away from her head at all angles, like a cartoon depiction of fright. The eyebrows she'd drawn in brown pencil arched thin and high, adding to the startled effect. Her gray-and-blue uniform looked itchy and hot. Her badge read ROSE PERSHING.

"We don't have a Sheriff Zanetta," she said, her wide eyes fixed on Maxey's face as if memorizing her for the police artist.

"My aunt said he was in charge of a murder investigation a few years ago."

"He probably was. How long ago was it?"

"Ten years."

Another female officer, looking through the bottom drawer of a well-stuffed file cabinet, raised her pink face to call, "He retired last year."

Maxey felt a swoop of frustration; she hadn't expected to run into a roadblock this quickly in her investigative journey. "Is there anyone else here I could talk to? Someone who would have been with the department then and maybe worked on that case?"

"We wouldn't have any way of knowing that," Rose said, folding her arms on the shelf of her bosom.

Rather than point out that of course there were ways of finding out, Maxey smiled hard. "Please, could you ask a few of the older deputies? It's very important."

"Why?"

The flushed-faced woman had apparently decided to stay out of further discussion. Pressing a stack of file folders to her chest, she exited, stage right.

Maxey leaned forward, lowering her voice, changing her smile for an expression that felt like pained earnestness. "My mother was murdered all those years ago, and her killer was never apprehended. I might have some new information."

Rose Pershing gave her five seconds more of hard scrutiny before turning away to punch a button, one of many in an electronic console on a desk. "Grue, could you come up front for a minute?"

The man who appeared seconds later wore a white shirt, gray slacks, and a necktie splotched with yellow and red flowers. Sixty, maybe sixty-five, he inspired some hope in Maxey.

Rose pulled him deeper into the office, away from the counter, and Maxey imagined she was explaining her version of the situation, a covering of that gray wool ass in case Maxey should turn out to be armed and dangerous.

The man went out another door and arrived beside Maxey. "I'm Sgt. Robert Gruder," he said, not offering to shake hands. "Can I help you?"

"Like the town?" She showed him a relaxed, friendly smile. "Your family must go way back."

He nodded, waiting for her to get to the point. His butch haircut and ice gray eyes matched his ramrod stance.

"My mother was shot ten years ago in Gruder. I wasn't around then, except for the funeral. All I know is that the murder wasn't solved. I'd like to talk to someone involved in the case, but I understand Sheriff Zanetta isn't with the department anymore."

"Let's sit down over here," Gruder said, stretching out an arm and hand like an usher, showing her to a row of mismatched chairs ranging along one wall. Settling two places down from Maxey, Gruder twisted side-saddle, his elbow on the chair back, his head on his fist. "Now, you are who?"

"Maxey Burnell, from Colorado. My mother was Peggy Witter Burnell."

His gaze flickered with recognition.

"Did you happen to work with Sheriff Zanetta on that case, Sergeant?"

"No, I didn't."

Again Maxey felt disappointment wash the starch out of her backbone. "Well, then whom could I—"

"I can give you Nolan's address. He won't mind a pretty young woman coming by to chat for a while."

"Great! That would be just great."

Sergeant Gruder took his time about finding a memo pad in his shirt pocket, then a pen. Finally, settling the former on one knee, he began to print letters on it with the latter. He ripped off the page and handed it over.

"Country View, south on Walnut to Bentwood," Maxey read. "A subdivision?"

"Nursing home," Gruder said, putting away his pen and pad.

■

The lobby of Country View Care Center was a big glass box lined with elderly people in easy chairs and on couches. Potted palms and rubber trees formed an island in the middle of the gray-tiled floor. Farther along, a smaller island reared up—a black-lacquered baby grand piano. A gnarled lady in a faded blue plaid dress sat on the matching bench, touching keys so carefully, no notes sounded.

Maxey strode past the gauntlet of seniors toward the reception desk at the far end, smiling indiscriminately at both the alert and the blankly staring faces. One old gentleman wearing a John Deere cap twisted his wheelchair to track her passage and called her Sherry. She waved and kept walking.

Reception was a six-foot-long chest-high counter. A stocky young woman in a white pantsuit looked up from a clipboard. "Help you?"

"Could I please see Nolan Zanetta?"

"Oh, I expect." She turned around as another woman in white came into the reception area. "Shirley, is Nolan in his room, you think?"

Shirley looked almost as old as her charges—old enough that she wore a traditional starched white cap on her blue-gray hair. "TV room, last I saw him."

The younger woman leaned forward to point. "Okay, you take this hall till it T's. Go right, and then on your left in a little bit you'll see a big room with chairs and a television set. If he isn't there, come back and we'll chase him down for you."

"Thanks."

Maxey plunged into the tunnel of hallway, where a hint of ammonia hung in the air. She passed a tiny, shuffling woman going in the opposite direction. The woman didn't look up, intent on holding to the wooden rail that jutted from the glossy blue wall.

Hunching her shoulders, trying not to get too good a look at anything through the open doors of rooms she passed, Maxey wondered if her mother's death was such a tragedy after all. Better a bullet blowing out everything in one quick breath than to outlive one's body and mind.

The television room, like the lobby, let in too much unflattering sun. A regiment of Danish Modern armchairs faced one dusty-screened twenty-seven-inch TV hanging from a wall bracket. It blared a frenetic game show.

Three wheelchairs were parked at odd angles, forming a straggly front row. The occupants turned to stare at her—all men, Maxey guessed, though one might have been a flat-chested woman with a bad haircut.

"Nolan Zanetta?" Maxey inquired brightly.

No one held up a hand.

"I'm looking for Nolan Zanetta." Her smile felt like paste hardening.

"What for?" demanded a bald man whose eyes glared in two different directions.

"Mr. Zanetta?" Maxey zeroed in on him. "Could I please ask you some questions about a case you worked when you were sheriff?"

The man deliberately straightened his chair away from her to gaze up at a contestant shaking hands with the host. Maxey's heart, already at low ebb, sank further. Sgt. Gruder had warned her not to expect much.

"What do you want to know?" The third man's voice was deep and carrying, the kind of voice that could encourage a criminal to come out with his hands up.

Maxey looked at him. He had Cary Grant's cleft chin, Tip O'Neill's fine spill of white hair, and Billy Joel's heavy-lidded eyes. A red plaid flannel shirt stretched across his slab shoulders and beefy chest. Even in advanced years and in a wheelchair, the man could be called a hunk.

"Are you Sheriff Zanetta?" Maxey asked, moving closer.

"Yeah, that's him," the bald man shouted without looking around again.

"I'm Maxey Burnell. My mother was Peggy Witter Burnell."

A glint of interest registered in Zanetta's eyes, and Maxey allowed herself to hope this trip would be worthwhile after all.

"Are you going to offer Nole his old job back?" the bald man asked a decibel above the television's whistles, gongs, and applause.

"Let's go somewheres else," Zanetta said, swinging his chair around and palming the wheels toward an outside door. "Open that."

"Is it okay? I mean, do we need to ask someone at the front desk—"

He jerked his head impatiently. "I pay enough for the privilege of living here. These people work for me, and I can do as I damn well please." He rammed the door with the chair's footrest, and Maxey hastened around him to push the release bar, imagining a silent alarm going off in an office somewhere.

Except for a brief hang-up on the sill, their exodus was smooth sailing as they moved down a gentle concrete ramp to the main side-walk that circled the building. The sheriff folded his long-boned hands in his lap and waited for Maxey to start pushing. The sun felt like hot butter on her bare arms. Zanetta leaned his head back, eyes shut, and inhaled a snuffly, wet breath.

For a few moments, they walked and rode in silence, grateful for a few minutes of unqualified peace.

Then Zanetta leaned to the right side of the chair and peered at the lawn. "Watch for four-leaf clovers."

"We'll have better luck if we watch for four-leaf dandelions. Could I ask you about my mother?"

He grunted. "It was a long time ago. What do you want to stir the pot for now?"

"I feel guilty I didn't stir it before. Actually, I just found out my father's alive, and my aunt is accusing him of the murder. I want to show her she's wrong."

"Is that—lessee—Jeanette?"

"Janet, yes."

The wheels of the chair clattered across a metal plate in the sidewalk. The south-facing windows of the nursing home reflected like golden mirrors.

"Janet. I went to school with her. She's got a big imagination. Do you have a cigarette?"

"Sorry, no."

"Not as sorry as I am." He coughed and canted sideways to spit at the grass.

"You didn't consider my father a suspect, then?"

"Who was your father?"

"Deon Burnell." She waited patiently while he processed the name through his outmoded data bank.

"I remember," Zanetta said. "He was a couple hundred miles away from the murder scene. In an auto race or sumpin'. He raced cars, you know."

"Is there anything about the case you can tell me that I won't find in the newspaper accounts?"

They reached the corner and made a bumpy turn over a pothole in the sidewalk. Zanetta's knees and feet flopped helplessly, his bare white ankles looking vulnerable below the cuffs of his brown twill trousers.

Maxey kept quiet, hoping he was thinking about that long-ago murder case and not about what he wanted for lunch. Eventually, his head began to bob toward his chest.

"So you were satisfied with Deon Burnell's alibi?" she asked too loudly and too brightly.

He shrugged.

"Sheriff, do you happen to know where Deon was living at that time? Or where he lives now?"

"Nope. Wait—let's see." He cocked his head, then shook it. "Nope."

They turned another corner and strolled along the shady north side of the building. In one window, a pale figure sitting on a bed waved at them. Across the street, a dog chained to a front porch barked two token warnings.

"Would you describe the murder scene for me?" Maxey prompted.

Zanetta made an effort to sit up straighter, wiping his mouth with the back of a spotted wrist. "She was head shot. One twenty-two-caliber bullet above the left eye from about ten feet away. The weapon was a rifle, recovered at the scene. Maple stock and brass butt plate and frame. All wiped clean."

Maxey nodded. She already knew that. She pictured two non-descript hands frantically scrubbing at the rifle with a handkerchief or a shirttail in the seconds before Janet should come galloping up on the back porch.

"It was fired from the hip," he continued. "Or else the shooter was sitting down. Bullet exited the top of her head." Zanetta scratched the top of his own head with a forefinger, the rest of his hand splayed like a broken spider.

Maxey swallowed around a knot in her throat. "Who do you think did it?"

"Wish I knew. Probably her lover."

"My mother didn't have a lover."

"Think she'd have told you if she did?"

"No, but—"

"She wasn't a bad-looking woman. Looked a little like June Lockhart with frown lines." He chuckled. "Modern woman like yourself, and you can't accept that Mama Patty would have a sex life?"

"Mama Peggy," Maxey corrected. "Are you sure you're remembering the right murder?"

He shifted impatiently in the chair, and it lurched forward. "That was the one and only murder I ever got while I was in the department. Sure would like to have solved it. Tried my damnedest."

Another corner, another turn, and Maxey trundled Zanetta steadily past the canopied entrance, expecting at any moment for someone in a uniform to come outside and ask her what she thought she was doing.

"Who was this alleged lover?" Maxey asked.

Zanetta brushed in front of his face to discourage a persistent fly. "Don't know."

"Did you ever know?" Maxey bit her lower lip, embarrassed about her tactless wording. "I mean, did anyone ever know?"

"Hell, I don't know."

"Please, Sheriff. I need somewhere to start."

"Look for a married man. That was my understanding."

Maxey, about to turn the chair on the last corner of the round-trip, came to a full, sudden stop, nearly pitching the old man out. It was difficult to apologize to him when anger and denial were swamping her control. Could her bitter, unhappy mother have been irresistible to any male, especially a married one? Would Peggy have committed adultery after her own husband had so disappointed her? Unbelievable.

She worked the right wheel free of the concrete fault it had hung up in and resumed walking.

"Sheriff, are you sure—"

"Goddamnit. Are you watching for four-leaf clovers or not?"

They returned through the same door they'd left. A different group of TV spectators sat staring at an ad for dog food.

"Thank you for your time," Maxey leaned over to murmur to the sheriff, lifting his hand and shaking it.

"Time's all I've got to give, and it's in precious short supply."

Feeling bad for him, for all of them, she nodded and hurried away.

At the reception desk, she stopped to speak again to the younger nurse. "Could you tell me about Nolan Zanetta? What's wrong with him?"

"Oh, my dear, what isn't? Are you a relative?"

"No, and I don't want to pry into his medical problems. It's just that I'm wondering how much of what he said to me could be true."

The nurse tapped her clipboard with her ballpoint pen, considering. "My estimate is ninety-nine and forty-four-one-hundredths percent. The rest is probably"—she put a hand backward beside her mouth and whispered—"bullshit."

When Maxey strode through the lobby, the same old gentleman called her Sherry, and the woman next to him asked in a hard-of-hearing bray, "You from the Future Senior Citizens of America, sweetheart?"

Maxey emerged under the front canopy and walked to the car, though she wanted to run.

Now what? She glanced at her watch before backing out of the parking place and dropping the gearshift into drive. There was still time to make Janet's sewing circle meeting—effect a dramatic surprise entrance and please the old girl.

Maybe one of her seamstress friends had known Peggy and would have some theory about who the alleged lover might be. But no, Janet would never forgive Maxey if she interrogated the little social gathering.

Driving slowly north into the outskirts of Fremont, Maxey considered what else she might do with her morning. She could stop at a news office or library and read microfilm about the murder investigation, but staring at a fuzzy screen till her head hurt didn't appeal. Besides, there would be nothing in a small-town newspaper report that she didn't already know or couldn't get from a primary source.

The question was, Who was primary?

She braked for a four-way stop, noticed a sign for frozen custard halfway up the side street, and signaled a turn in that direction. A strawberry milk shake would help her think straight.

She rolled the Escort toward the white shack plastered with menu signs, bumped over the low curb into a gravel lot, and circled the building, looking for the drive-up window. On the far side, on neighboring property beside a colorless metal shed, hunkered a bright red car. It sported a black roll cage, cutout fenders, and a lot of printing on the side and hood: CAMARO. 55. RED LINE OIL. SNAP-ON TOOLS.

Feeling as if a ray of sunlight had just reached down to spotlight the stock car for her, Maxey veered in that direction and parked the Escort. The dust she'd aroused settled back to the gravel before she got out, slammed the door, and crossed the dirt and weed boundary between the Custard Castle and Serves-U-Rite Garage.

. . .

Two gas pumps sat in front of a steep-roofed white one-room office. Behind that, a grimy concrete-block garage rose out of the litter of tires, barrels, and parts of cars surrounding it. An air wrench whined from one of the two open garage doors.

Maxey paused beside the stock car, not touching it as she studied the all-aluminum interior. Then she followed the sound of the wrench.

A young man in tattered blue denim coveralls stood under a maroon sedan on a lift in the middle of the concrete floor. When Maxey shouted, "Hello," he ducked his head to look at her.

"Help you?" he asked, resting the wrench on his shoulder.

"May I ask you about car fifty-five out there? I'd like to talk to the owner."

"Yeah? It's not for sale." He smiled uncertainly, his teeth dazzling white in the black of his beard and grease-smeared face.

"I don't want to buy it. I want to ask the driver if he's heard of another driver—someone I'm trying to find."

"Oh. Owe you money?"

She shook her head. "A long-lost relative."

"Your deadbeat husband?"

"No, no." She laughed. "You must have had some bad experiences to be so suspicious."

He left the shelter of the sedan to put the wrench on a workbench and wipe his hands on an oily red rag. Nodding at the driveway, he said, "It's my car. What do you want to know?"

"Where around here do you race it?"

"A-Plus Speedway, usually. South of Norfolk."

"Ever heard of a driver named Deon Burnell? Dee Burnell?"

He stroked his face with the back of a hand as he considered. "Don't think so. What's he drive?"

"I have no idea."

"Superstock, though?"

"Uh, I don't know."

To his credit, the man didn't snort or roll his eyes.

Maxey raised her hands, palms up. "I guess I wasn't thinking straight. I saw your car and thought you'd know my dad. . . ." Her confession trailed off to nothing—like what she had gained from bothering this poor mechanic.

"Your dad, huh? How old a guy?"

"Late fifties."

"Did he grow up around here?"

"Yes, but then he moved to Ohio, and after that, he could have gone anywhere."

"Tommy Coffman might know."

"Yeah? How do I find Tommy Coffman?"

"Come in the office. I've got his number, I think."

Maxey followed him through a connecting door into the closet-sized front building. The walls were festooned with fan belts and hubcaps, the glass counter stuffed with wiper blades, spray-paint cans, and candy bars. The floor was a narrow pathway between soft-drink machines, stacks of batteries, and cardboard dumps full of car accessories. It smelled of gasoline and strong coffee.

"Want a cup?" her guide asked, sorting through a pile of gritty-looking invoices till he uncovered a flip-up address minder.

"No, thanks. Is this Tommy Coffman a race driver?"

"Yeah. Past president of the SCCA. Tours all over the country, knows everybody. Oh, that's Sports Car Club of America, to you."

"Sounds great. I really appreciate this."

He ripped off a piece of cash-register tape and wrote on the back of it with a nubbin of pencil. Maxey checked to be sure she could make out the phone number before sticking out her right hand for a hearty shake. His fingers felt as rough and hard as limestone.

"Want to use my phone?" he offered.

"Oh, gosh, I sure would. I've got a calling card if it's long distance."

"He lives up at West Point. Help yourself." And he walked back to the garage, leaving her alone in the office with all that inventory and the cash register and an open line to the world.

Maxey dialed quickly, then put her free hand in her jeans pocket, where it couldn't be accused of anything.

"Hello. Coffman."

He answered so fast, she hadn't time to rehearse her opening lines. "Hi. Tommy Coffman, is it?"

"Speaking. Who's this?"

"Maxey Burnell. You don't know me, but don't hang up. I'm not selling anything."

"Okay," he said, sounding reasonably interested.

"I was told by a stock-car driver that you might know my father. His name's Deon Burnell."

"Yes?"

" 'Yes,' you know him?"

" 'Yes,' I might."

"I'm trying to locate him."

"Why?"

Maxey huffed an exasperated breath. "Can't a daughter want to say hello to her father that she hasn't seen in quite a while? Maybe give him a hug?"

"It's possible. Why haven't you seen him for a while?"

"Because I thought he was dead."

"Oh. Uh-huh. That would explain it. He thought you were dead, too?"

"Look, Mr. Coffman, if you have any idea how I could contact him, I'd appreciate it. If you don't, then I won't bother you anymore."

"You want to go with me to a race tomorrow, we might see him. Can't guarantee anything."

"No kidding? That would be—where should I meet you?"

A car horn at the frozen-custard stand tapped out "Shave and a haircut, two bits." Young voices shouted questions and other young voices gave guffawing answers.

"My house," Coffman said. "Where you calling from now?"

"The Serves-U-Rite Garage. In Fremont."

"Okay. Macko there can tell you how to get to my place south of West Point."

"What time tomorrow should I be there?"

"No later than six—A.M."

The receiver was getting sweaty. Maxey switched hands to rub the damp one on her thigh. "Where is this race?"

"Steamboat Springs."

Maxey smiled. "We have a Steamboat Springs in Colorado, too."

"That's the one."

"You want me to go to Colorado with you?" she yelped.

"No. You want to go with me," Coffman reminded her patiently.

"How will we get to Steamboat?"

"My Cessna one eighty-five Skywagon. You can chip in on the gas—if you still want to go."

"Your house at six," she answered crisply, then thanked him before disconnecting. She could check up on him that afternoon and cancel her reservation if she uncovered rape or murder in his resumé.

She interrupted Macko's labors again to ask directions to Coffman's place. He sketched her a messy map using a Magic Marker on paper toweling.

"Look for the wind sock," he advised.

"So would you trust your sister to fly cross-country with this man?" she asked, folding the towel to fit her purse.

"Sure. He's a good pilot."

"No, I mean is he a good—"

An engine roared into the side yard and they both turned to look at a white van rocking to a rabbit stop. It disgorged two hairy young men, both of whom hailed Macko by name and immediately engaged him in conversation about throttle and sway-bar control cables.

Shouting, "Thanks again," Maxey withdrew to buy a strawberry shake and consume it in her plain vanilla Ford.

■

The Timely Stitchers still plied their needles when Maxey returned to the farmhouse shortly after noon. A few of the ladies were standing, gathering belongings, when Maxey walked into the living room, but they all sat down again and looked at her expectantly.

Janet clapped her hands and announced to everybody over the good-natured din that this was Maxey, and everybody smiled and nodded.

"Goodness, what a nice big group," Maxey gushed. She'd promised herself not to use Aunt Janet's friends to further her own investigative ends. But the temptation of easy pickings here assembled was too great. "Are you all from Gruder?" She made a mental note of the twin sisters who hailed from West Point.

Twenty minutes later, when the two stood up to go, their matching tapestry bags fat with quilt squares under their arms, Maxey followed them out to their car.

The day had vacillated between partly cloudy and partly sunny. At the moment, the latter had won out, making the damp grass steam and smell of compost.

The twins wobbled through the yard on their white high heels, their ankles as insubstantial as chicken bones. The hemlines of their similar but not matching pink dresses hung badly out of true. One sister wore her hair in a frizzy upsweep that glittered with enough pins, barrettes, and combs to wipe out a small notions counter. The other sister had cut hers like a wedge-shaped lamp shade.

Maxey held the passenger door of their silver Cadillac as twin one heaved her quilting and herself inside. Twin two settled in to drive, her long, bony legs stretching to reach the pedals.

"Do you ladies happen to know Tommy Coffman?" Maxey asked, leaning on the sill of the open window while seat belts clicked into place.

"Everyone knows Tommy," one said as the other nodded.

"Would you give him a good character reference? He's offered to give me a ride that I need, and I don't know a thing about him."

The sisters consulted each other—eyes only, no words exchanged.

"He does talk a lot about cars," one said.

"And airplanes," said the other.

"But he's a good, honest, churchgoing gentleman?" Maxey coached.

"I don't think he goes to church," one sister said, and the other added, "He's probably as honest as he needs to be." The sister nearest to Maxey beamed up at her. "*Good* is such a relative term." The other twin started the Caddy, foot heavy on the gas, and rammed it into gear.

Maxey jumped back as the tires spun in the slippery grass, caught, and launched the Cadillac across the yard. It eased to the right at the entrance to let Scotty's red Bronco turn in off the road. The Bronco bobbed slowly up the driveway, passed Maxey, and kept going, Scotty waving grandly. He ran it into the grass at the southwest corner of the house, hopped out, and whistled his way to the hatch door to unload a posthole digger and a bag of cement.

"Hi," Maxey said, walking to join him. "You're making progress."

Scotty hauled out two metal cross-armed posts and dropped them clanking to the ground. "Oh, we're going to have a fine clothes dryer out here in no time."

"Scotty, do you happen to know Tommy Coffman from up near West Point?"

He paused to consider, fingering his bristly jaw. "Tommy Coffman. Right. Has his own airstrip behind his barn."

"That's the fella. I'm thinking about flying back to Colorado with him for a couple of days. Do you know any reason I shouldn't?"

Scotty gave her a squinty one-eyed glance. "Because your auntie will throw a supervainglorious fit if you run off when you no sooner got here?" he hazarded.

Maxey grimaced. She decided that was enough of trying to be careful about accepting rides from strangers. After all, Tommy Coffman didn't know anything about her, so the odds were even. Right?

A crowd of the sewing ladies emerged on the back porch, apparently deserting en masse. They eased arthritic joints down the steps, milled toward their vehicles, and called their good-byes. Nodding and waving, Maxey moved against the grain, reached the porch, and stepped into the cool, dim kitchen.

Janet twitched around from her place at the sink to see who had come in. She rinsed a handful of drinking glasses in water hot enough to send up steam.

"What can I do to help?" Maxey asked, cravenly stalling off the news of her Colorado side trip.

Janet uncovered a colander from a stack of pans on the counter.

"Take this and get us some green beans for supper. Pick one of the middle rows. Mind, your shoes will get muddy. I'm going to run to the grocery for some pork chops. Does that sound good? You eat pork, don't you?"

"Afraid so. Get the low-fat kind."

"I don't believe they have low-fat—oh, you! You're teasing me." Janet grabbed up her black pocketbook from the table. "Did you find out anything this morning at Fremont?"

"I'm not sure," Maxey admitted. "Probably not." She couldn't let this perfect opening go by. "I did get a lead on my dad, though. I hate to tell you, but I'll be flying to Colorado in the morning for a couple of days."

Janet stared at her. "You're going home?"

"No. To Steamboat Springs. There's a race there over the weekend that Deon might attend."

"Seems kind of silly to me," Janet said mildly. "Fly all the way to Nebraska. Fly all the way to Colorado. Fly all the way to Nebraska. Fly all the way to Colorado."

"Well, I know, but it's too good an opportunity to pass up. I've heard of this Steamboat race. It's like a grand prix of vintage cars—around the streets of town. If I don't go, it'll be another year till the next one."

Janet set down her purse and put her fists on her hips. "What makes you think he's going to be there?"

"Tommy Coffman—do you know Tommy Coffman?"

"I'd recognize him on the street."

"I guess Dad drove—Deon drives"—Maxey frowned; neither version felt natural in her mouth—"vintage cars."

"What is that? A Model T?"

"I'm not sure. I guess I'll find out."

Janet sniffed once, hard, and stuffed her purse under her arm again. Patting her bangs into place, she headed outside. Slipping off her tennis shoes and toeing them out of the way under a chair, Maxey followed.

"Well, after the race, you ought to just stay in Colorado," Janet threw over her shoulder. "Save yourself a lot of trouble and expense."

"No! I want to spend some time here with you. This little two-day commute isn't going to cost much, because I'll be going in Tommy Coffman's private plane."

Janet flapped a hand in dismissal as she marched toward the barn garage. Maxey sighed. Janet hadn't thrown a supervainglorious fit, but she was obviously a notch short of miffed.

Swinging the colander, Maxey walked past Scotty, who had scraped the grass away from his chosen spot and was beginning to work the posthole digger into the dirt. Around the corner, behind the house, the garden stretched far and wide, neat rows of sweet corn, cabbages, and onions on one side, an unruly jumble of tomato vines on the other. Pleased with herself for recognizing the green bean plants, Maxey located the approximate center row and squatted beside it.

Warm brown soil squeezed up around her bare toes. Leaves and insects tickled her arms; sweat trickled between her breasts and behind her knees. She was vaguely aware of a car starting, choking off, and voices raised in minor argument. Then Janet stomped around the corner of the house.

"My car won't start. Can I borrow yours?"

"Sure. The keys are on the dresser in my bedroom. I'll get them for you."

"No, I'll do it. I can't drive Scotty's Bronco because it has stick shift."

"No problem. The Escort is an automatic."

"I sometimes take Curtis's car, but he's not home."

"It's okay. Really."

"I'll be careful."

Maxey laughed. "Go already."

Compressing her lips, Janet hurried off. The back porch door banged and after a minute banged again. A motor revved, and Maxey's rental, presumably, muttered off into the distance.

Maxey relaxed in the saunalike sun, wrapping her hands around eight, ten beans at a time and pulling them free. Birds chattered in the trees. Scotty's posthole digger echoed off the barn—*whump, whump, whump.*

When the colander was heaped so full that beans kept sliding off, Maxey carried it out to the end of the row, one hand splayed protectively over the top. She couldn't remember how long it had been since she'd walked barefoot on thick silky grass. Impulsively, she set down the beans and sat beside them, digging her toes into the cool green. Seduced by the scent of clover, she put her head on her knees and dozed, like Dorothy in the poppies.

■

"Okay if I go on in?" a male voice shouted.

Scotty's voice answered something Maxey didn't catch.

A metal door banged, and then shoes crunched gravel. After a moment, feet hit the porch floor and the screen door slapped.

Pushing herself up off the ground, brushing at her seat and discovering it had soaked up all the moisture in a square foot of grass, Maxey retrieved the colander. She walked around the house, to find Scotty mixing lumpy gray cement in a dented gray wheelbarrow. He'd stripped off his shirt, and his bare back and arms and brow gleamed and dripped. A green garden hose ran water sluggishly over the toes of his battered brown boots. As his shovel folded water into the grit, the sound took Maxey back to her childhood—*shoosh, shoosh, shoosh*—on a day when her dad installed a post for a tetherball that she played with maybe five times in her life.

Her mother had worried Maxey might get tangled up and hang herself.

A white van was parked by the back porch. A painting of a rainbow arched from front wheel well to back wheel well, and raindrops below the arch artfully formed the words CLOUD-SOF-WATER.

Maxey strolled close enough to Scotty to converse, but not close enough to be splattered by the beads of cement that speckled his baggy white jeans. "Anything I can do to help you?" she offered.

"When I get this ready, you can hold the post up straight while I shovel in around it, thank 'ee kindly."

"You look as if you know what you're doing there." She set the colander down and folded her arms.

"Done it before, that's for sure. Worked for a sidewalk contractor when I was just out of high school—the Good Intentions Pavement Company."

When Maxey laughed, he paused in his labor long enough to lay a work-gloved hand on his white-haired chest. "Cross my heart."

"What occupation did you retire from?"

"All of them."

Maxey snickered. "You know what I mean. What did you do for a living most of your life?"

He stooped to pick up the hose and squirt the mix for a second or two. "Well, my last job was reading water meters in Denver."

"Hey, you didn't tell me you'd lived in Colorado."

"Colorado, Wyoming, California, Indiana, Michigan, Texas— you want me to go on? Colorado's one of my favorites, though. All that calendar-photo scenery."

"You can come back and stay at the Burnell Tourist Home anytime. I'll bet Janet has never been that far west. She'd love it. Did you read meters in all those states?"

He shook his head, gave the cement one last turn, and straightened, one hand in the small of his back. "Drove a milk truck, clerked in a hardware store, delivered pizza, washed windows, washed dishes, washed cars."

"Tolkien said that if a man wandered, it didn't mean he was lost."

"Thanks," he said. "That's one I hadn't heard."

Scotty tossed the shovel on top of the barrow, then wheeled it next to the hole he'd dug. Lifting one metal cross-armed post out of the grass, he let it thud into the hole, checked it for height, pulled it up an inch, and motioned for Maxey to hold it upright while he shoveled cement.

A man in a white cap, white overalls, and white gym shoes breezed out of the kitchen door, waving as he walked, and hopped into the van to drive away.

"Never went to college, though," Scotty continued. "Never tried a lot of things I'd like to have tried."

"Like what?"

"Flying an airplane and jumping out of one. Sight-seeing in Africa and South America. When I was a kid, I wanted to be a foreign correspondent. Travel the world and write about it."

"Not too late."

Scotty grunted. He stabbed the point of his shovel up and down in the filling hole. "I'm past my salad days and working on dessert."

Maxey felt the cement begin to take the weight of the pole away from her, and she renewed her effort to hold it straight. Scotty backed away and circled her, checking the angle.

"Pull it half a whisker toward you," he said, and began shoveling again. "So, do you plan to be a newspaperwoman all your life?"

"Something wrong with that?"

"No. Long as you enjoy it."

"I do. Except for soliciting advertisers. And dunning the ones that don't pay. And having to think up a new editorial subject every week. And never getting Wednesday off. And fighting with the printer over—"

"I can see you enjoy it, all right."

Maxey laughed. "The list of likes is longer than the list of gripes. Isn't that about the best you can expect out of any job?"

"You can let go now."

Caught up in the discussion, Maxey had to think a moment about what Scotty meant. Then she carefully loosened her fingers from the pole and retreated a step. The pole continued to stand steady and almost straight.

"It's leaning this way," she said.

"I want her to, a little, because the clotheslines will tense her the other way. Sometimes we have to lean over backward to appear to be straight. That's me talking."

They paused for lemonade that felt cold all the way down into Maxey's chest, and then they planted another crossbarred pole twelve feet from the first. They were standing back to admire their handiwork when the Ford Escort roared in off the highway and sped toward them as if the driveway had turned into the A-Plus Speedway. It scattered Maxey and Scotty, crushed the colander, and braked just short of a poplar tree, which seemed to shiver in relief. The motor dieseled for a couple seconds and died.

Maxey rushed to the driver's side, where Janet sat as rigid as a crash-test dummy, staring through the windshield, knuckles white on the steering wheel. Wrenching open the door, Maxey let out a tide of air-conditioned cold.

"Are you okay?" she asked her aunt, sensing that Scotty had come up behind to lean with her to look inside the car.

"He tried to kill me," Janet said in a soft, matter-of-fact way before touching her head to the steering wheel and weeping with all the stops out.

"I decided to go to the Hy-Vee supermarket in Fremont for my groceries. So I got them and I started home," Janet said, swiping at her rosy nose with a paper tissue.

The three of them sat in the kitchen, Janet clutching Scotty's hand on the tabletop. In the dim quiet, Janet's story sounded like something to be told around a campfire. When the cat brushed surreptitiously against Maxey's leg, she jumped as if she'd been slapped.

"I noticed this truck in my rearview mirror, but I didn't think anything about it. Who would? Trucks are behind you every day."

"What kind of truck?" Scotty asked.

Janet shrugged. "Your usual kind—cab, flatbed, pickup. Black, I think, but maybe really dark blue or brown. I hate it when somebody's following close, breathing down your trunk. So when I got to the Bramburger place, I pulled over crossways on their lane to let him pass, and he did. Disappeared over the next rise, and I thought no more about it until—"

She squirmed up straighter, beginning to progress from fright to anger. "Until I passed the Starett place, and there was what looked like the same truck, parked across *their* lane. Soon as I was past him, he pulled out and tailed me like a dog sniffing another dog. Before I could get my mad up to speed, I came to the Jonkey Bridge."

Janet coughed and blew her nose and coughed some more. Maxey banged a knee on the table leg, hurrying to get her a glass of lemonade.

"It's an iron bridge, Maxey," Janet finally continued. "The old-fashioned narrow kind with the guardrail approaches and overhead girders."

Maxey nodded. Janet patted at Scotty's arm, as if he was the one needing comfort.

"There wasn't anything coming from the other way, so I moved over left, ready to fly right down the center of the bridge, and that's when the truck behind me blew his horn a long, arrogant blast and proceeded to speed up like he was going to pass me on the left. Well, of course there wasn't room to pass—we were almost to the bridge. I didn't know whether to accelerate or slam on the brakes. While I was trying to decide, the truck squeezed up next to me and crowded me toward the upcoming guardrail. I was going to run smack into the end of it, head-on, at fifty miles an hour."

Shaking her head in horror, Maxey looked at Scotty. He stared at the tablecloth, face blank of emotion, as if already planning how to find the mystery truck and press charges against the driver.

"By rights, I should be roadkill right now," Janet said. "I slammed on the brakes, and the car kind of fishtailed, and the truck went whooshing on through the bridge, and I finally got stopped broadside halfway through the bridge, and I've got no idea in the world how I got there without so much as a scratch on me or your car, Maxey."

Maxey stood up again to lean over Janet with an awkward hug.

Janet stiffened in the embrace. "Oh, dear, maybe I'm mistaken about the car. He might have scraped up against me on the driver's side. Oh, Maxey, I'll pay for any damages."

"Don't be silly. It's insured."

Scotty pushed up from the table. "I'll take a look."

The women followed him outside, heads down, discussing.

"It's got to be someone under the influence of alcohol," Maxey said. "Some idiot with a head start on happy hour."

"No." Janet sounded positive. "He didn't weave around. And a drunk wouldn't have stopped and waited for me like he did."

"You keep calling the driver 'he.' You're sure it was a man?"

"It could have been a chimpanzee, for all I saw. I was too busy saving my skin."

"So you don't know if there was more than one person in the truck?"

"Maybe no one was in the truck. Maybe it was like that malignant car in the Stephen King story."

"Malevolent, you mean," Maxey said, laughing, glad that her aunt's sense of humor was taking charge.

They'd reached the yard, where Scotty had squatted to sight along the white Ford's left flank. He brushed his fingers over it, rose, and circled to inspect the front bumper.

"I hope you do find some dark paint on it," Maxey said. "Then we'll know what color the truck is. It would be nice to have at least one clue to give the police."

"Oh, there's no use calling the sheriff," Janet declared. "What could they do? Take down my teaspoonful of information and laugh as soon as I leave?"

"Well, I admit there isn't much for them to go on, but they ought to have the report, just in case it happens to someone else sometime. Maybe it already has happened to someone else." Maxey bent to look closer at a black smear by the rear wheel well, but it was only mud.

"I don't think it was random, Maxey, and I don't think it was a drunk driver. It was someone deliberately attacking this particular car." Janet spaced and emphasized each word like a politician making a campaign promise. "But I was the wrong driver."

Scotty gave his head one quick negative jerk and moved around to the other side of the Escort.

Maxey shook her head, too. "Come on, Janet. You don't really think—"

Janet lifted her chin. "I certainly do. Here you come breezing into Gruder, stirring up the peace, asking questions about an old-news murder. No one ever tried to kill me before. It was your car. I rest my case."

"You have long red hair. I have short blond hair. So you're saying we should look for someone with a dark pickup and lousy eyesight."

"Although, maybe I was the target, come to think of it. Villains always go after loved ones of the detective who's snooping too close."

"So now we're on the lookout for a bad guy who's read too many murder mysteries."

"I have my own idea about who we're on the lookout for. Ask me, you could save yourself a trip to Colorado, because the fugitive you want must be right here."

Maxey threw both hands up. "Can you really picture my dad skulking around Nebraska back roads in a depraved pickup truck? Don't you think he's got better things to do?"

Janet sniffed. "You just be careful, Maxey Diane Burnell. I'd dearly hate to be proven correct."

Scotty gave the right side of the Ford a cursory examination, and the rear even less. He left them without comment, striding away to yank up his shovel, the empty cement bags, and the posthole digger. He slammed everything into the wheelbarrow and marched toward the barn, his neck scarlet with sunburn and, no question, anger.

Janet spread her hands over her ears. "Gracious! I left the pork chops in the trunk."

Maxey pulled the key out of the ignition and they retrieved three sacks of groceries.

"I'll pick another batch of beans," Maxey said.

Janet nudged the mangled colander with one sandaled foot. "That could have been me," she observed with forlorn melodrama.

■

"All the eggs broke. I'm going next door to borrow some," Janet called up the back stairs after Maxey, who was on her way to wash after a second excursion in the garden.

"Okay."

The heat trapped in the top of the house settled around Maxey like a cloud. In the bathroom, she scrubbed her hands and rinsed her sweaty face at the chipped white sink. The room had been papered when flocked patterns were in style. A furry gold trellis crisscrossed green ivy that almost matched the green felt carpet. It was all about the size of a walk-in closet, which it undoubtedly was when the house was first built.

She finished patting her face dry and hung up the towel, her movements slow and thoughtful. Was Janet right? Had the truck driver been sober and stone-cold set on running her off the road because he thought she was snoop niece Maxey?

Vaguely conscious of voices and an occasional bump or bang downstairs, Maxey consulted with her reflection in the mirror of the medicine cabinet. On the other hand, could the driver have known exactly what he was doing? Could there be someone who wanted her sweet little old aunt dead? The idea would have seemed ridiculous except that there was no question someone had wanted Janet's sister dead ten years ago.

Maxey ran downstairs, her bare feet thumping on the wood risers. Hunting out a clean bowl, she carried it and the paper bag of green beans toward the sounds in the living room.

The front door yawned wide to the porch. A wasp zoomed in the open air between inside and out, crossed the boundary, and sailed to the foyer ceiling to explore corners.

Curtis and his friend Lance knelt beside the screen door, which lay flat on the middle of the carpet. Catching sight of Maxey, Lance leaned back and Curtis misfired a staple into the freshly stretched screen wire.

"Damn it, Lance. Hold it still, can't you?" Curtis fought the curling screen into place, jammed the gun against it, and fired another staple.

"Hi, guys." Maxey sat down in the dining room doorway and arranged her work in front of her.

Lance pushed up to his feet. "I gotta go, Curt."

"What are you doing tonight?" Curtis squeezed the trigger again.

Lance, sidestepping Maxey, didn't answer. Moments later, he tooled out of the driveway. Maxey caught a glimpse of bright red convertible.

"Is it my breath?" she asked, breaking the first bean in thirds.

Curtis considered his handiwork. "What?"

"Lance never wants to talk to me. Runs off like I'm Typhoid Maxey."

"That's just the way he is—kind of shy."

Maxey thought that made the boys two of a kind.

He stopped studying the door to glance at Maxey's face. "You look a lot like her."

Maxey had to blink a couple of times, getting her bearings. "Who? My mother?" If he thought that, it was because too much time had passed since he saw Peggy. Maxey didn't think she looked anything like her mother.

But at the moment, her forehead pinched in a frown, she felt like her. "You can't really remember her. You were a little kid when she was here."

"I guess I don't remember her very well," he agreed. "Except for how she looked"—he visibly swallowed—"that day."

"Finding her like that must have been a terrible shock for you."

"It was. Awful."

His voice cracked like an adolescent's, and Maxey felt a rush of sympathy for the child exposed to violent death. Jumping up, Curtis wrestled the screen door upright and manhandled it into the foyer.

"Can I help you there?" Maxey said, rubbing the heel of one hand across her eyes.

"No," he said brusquely. He put his back to her while he struggled to realign the hinges.

Maxey thought he really could use some help, but she also could see that he was set against hers. She concentrated on snapping green beans into uniform lengths.

Supper, when the time arrived, was fit for a king, if the king wasn't worried about his cholesterol: cornmeal-battered pork chops, mashed potatoes and gravy, green beans steamed with bits of onion and bacon, deviled eggs, baking soda biscuits, and chocolate pudding for dessert. The party of four ate heartily but mostly in silence, tired from the afternoon's activities and worried about Janet's misadventure.

■

The room glowed with silvery moonlight, and if Maxey stretched past the edge of the mattress, she could see the source, almost full, as three-dimensional as a new dime.

She'd been yawning and drooping while she sat with Janet and Scotty in front of CNN news, but by the time she'd brushed her teeth and changed into her Save the Whales nightshirt, she wasn't sleepy anymore.

Determined not to lie awake worrying about her father or her mother, she worried about the *Regard* instead.

Did she really believe that Reece could put out two issues in two weeks all on his own? He'd have to work overtime, and that would be a first in itself. If he let Clark help him, he'd be so busy telling the new man what to do, his work would probably be doubled instead of halved. On the plus side, maybe Clark would bring in some new accounts, selling advertising to shoe stores and podiatrists.

"Sell your share of the paper to me," Maxey had said to Reece the day after their Rev Taylor dinner. "I want to buy you out."

"With what?"

"That's the trouble. It would have to be an installment arrangement."

"Yeah? How much could you pay a month?"

"I need to do some figuring, but—fifty bucks?"

"Do you realize how long it would take you to pay me off? I'd be dead, and I don't expect to have any heirs to inherit the payments."

"How much money are we talking here, Reece? How much has Clark agreed to?"

"Not that I have to disclose it to you, but I'm too pleased with myself to keep it a secret. Twenty thousand dollars."

If Maxey had been standing, she'd have had to sit down. Since she was sitting down, she had to stand up. "Twenty–you liar!"

Reece shook his head, grinning. Canary feathers should have been leaking past his teeth.

"God, Reece. Why didn't you tell me Clark was buying lock, stock, and coffeepot, my share as well as yours? Is there an interstate highway scheduled to go through the building? A gold mine in the basement? What?"

"Clark sees a lot of potential here."

Maxey stared around the scruffy office. It looked like a garage sale without the racks of used clothing. "Forty thousand dollars of potential? The man is an idiot. And you expect me to treat him like an equal?"

"Come on, Maxey. You know that if our roles were reversed, you'd take the money and run."

"And that's how we'd repay Jim's ghost for trusting us with his newspaper? Fine. You leave. I'll leave. I won't even sell my share; I'll just walk away. You know Clark couldn't make a go of it without me. You take his money and watch the *Regard* sink like the *Titanic.* Let it be on your head."

"I'll be in Alaska. I won't see it sink."

"But you'll know. It'll haunt you. *I'll* haunt you. So will Jim."

"Okay, okay. Give me a contract to consider."

"How about a discount on the purchase price, my being your ex-wife and all?"

"Are you kidding? Being my ex-wife makes the price higher."

Before drawing up an agreement for Reece to, no doubt, reject, Maxey ran a discreet notice in the *Regard* classified section, soliciting a business partner. The advertisement didn't net a single inquiry, probably because it was so discreet, it was unintelligible.

She decided not to draw up a purchase contract for Reece to consider. Although she loved the newspaper, she wasn't willing to go down with it if it did indeed founder.

Like the predictable moon, Clark seemed inevitable.

Flopping over onto her stomach, Maxey resolutely shut her eyes. She'd think about it, Scarlett-style, tomorrow.

■

But the next day, she was too busy packing the smaller black bag and filling a thermos with coffee to think about the *Regard.* Armed with Macko's directions, Maxey set out for Tommy Coffman's place before the rest of the household was up.

She took the back way toward West Point, through Snyder, which might have been a ghost town as it slept in the predawn fog. The road doglegged east and north again around a cornfield rustling to itself. The ground fog broke apart and trailed away in wisps. A coyote or a skinny dog trotted out of the side ditch, changed his mind, and slithered out of sight in the weeds again.

The dark, empty landscape would have been the perfect place for a murder.

Maxey was so busy watching for iron bridges and pickup trucks, she almost missed Tommy Coffman's lane, marked by a black-and-white-checkered mailbox on a post made from an airplane propeller. She turned in, her headlights sweeping a soybean field before settling on the two-lane blacktopped driveway lined with bricks. Impressed already, she strained to see the house, but, as Macko had said, the lane was a long'un. At fifteen miles per hour, it took three minutes to reach the floodlit parking apron beside a six-car garage.

The house, what she could see of it in the growing light of morning, was disappointing. Not much bigger than the detached garage, it crouched low in a shaggy stand of juniper bushes, no lights showing. Somewhere in the back, a dog with a voice like an Uzi issued warning salvos.

Maxey parked on the concrete apron, well away from any of the closed garage doors. Grabbing up her overnight bag and the thermos, she stepped out into the soft, sweet-smelling air and twisted to look at the house again.

"This way." The hail came from straight ahead, between house and garage.

Jiggling her bag for a better grip, Maxey followed the voice and a narrow sidewalk into the backyard—an immense backyard comprised of one picnic table, one barbecue pit, one chain-link-fenced swimming pool, one chain-link-fenced dog, perhaps five trees, one airplane hangar, one airplane, and a mowed field that stretched farther than the morning light quite reached.

"Too early for a Jesus pusher, so you must be our passenger." Scarcely glancing at her, the man flicked away the cigarette he'd been smoking and walked toward the scarlet-and-white plane.

Maxey's first impression was shoulders. Dressed in blue chinos, a shiny blue windbreaker, and dazzling white tennis shoes, he was built a lot like Richard Chalmers, except smaller, an economy-sized wrestler. His heavy face was almost the same color as his wavy red hair. He reached the wing and wiggled a flap.

"I really appreciate your letting me come along," Maxey raised her voice to say as he circled the plane, testing various parts.

"First blind date he's had in years," another voice said at her shoulder, making her whirl in surprise. "He got real lucky all of a sudden."

The man belonging to the voice had a narrow, friendly face with a mouth full of large white teeth—so full, it didn't quite close when he shut it.

"Hello." Maxey backed away a few steps, ostensibly to make room to offer a handshake. "I'm Maxey Burnell."

"I know. We met."

"We did?"

"Yesterday." He grinned alarmingly, even his upper gum showing.

Maxey hated coy games like this, but she was definitely a captive audience until she got a place on that plane. "Where was that?"

"You mean you don't remember? You sure know how to hurt a guy."

Speaking of which, she longed to sock him right in the smirk. "Come on. Just tell me."

"Your house. Your aunt's house, I mean. Think about it."

Unwillingly, she thought about it. "The van with the rainbow?"

"Ri-i-ight. I'm your Cloud-Sof man."

"Water-softener service," she said, although she'd also thought of toilet paper.

"Ri-i-ight."

"Isn't it a little early to be out calling on clients?"

He bent over to laugh, giving Maxey a good view of his male-pattern baldness. "I'm Francis Coffman. I'm going to Steamboat, too."

For a weak moment, Maxey wondered if she really wanted to find her father today. "I see. Tommy's brother?"

"Guess again."

"Why don't you just tell me."

"Son." He glanced at the plane and, receiving some signal from Tommy, swooped to pick up Maxey's bag. "Shall we go, madame?"

She'd been a little worried about hitching a ride to Steamboat with a stranger. And rightly so. Francis was stranger than she'd imagined. Nevertheless, she shouldered her oversized purse, fat with writing materials, and boldly followed where she had never gone before—into the cockpit of a light plane.

■

Tommy's red-roofed barn passed under her right hip, every weathered shingle as clear as the back of her own hand locked on the arm of the seat. The engine roared incessantly, covering any sobs she might let slip.

The plane straightened up and set out for Colorado. From the corner of her eye, Maxey watched Tommy's stubby, freckled fingers adjust knobs, tap gauges, and relax on the bottom of the steering wheel. Having successfully launched them into the sky, he reached to retrieve a white captain's hat from the top of the control panel. Adjusting it low on his ruddy forehead, he settled back to enjoy the flight.

Francis, in the seat behind Maxey, leaned forward to yell in her ear. "Have you ever been to Steamboat Springs?"

"Not for a race. Have you?"

"Lots of times."

"Are you a driver?"

He guffawed. "I've got too much sense, s-e-n-s-e, and not enough cents, c-e-n-t-s."

"Are you going to race at Steamboat, Mr. Coffman?"

Tommy shook his head. "Getting too old."

Francis slapped the back of Maxey's seat. "Lost his nerve, he means. Never too old. Jessie Howsterman is seventy-eight and still racing—still winning."

"It's a sport for the young at heart," Tommy said.

"Boys with arrested development," Francis clarified.

Maxey stole a look at Tommy, wondering how he felt about Francis's clumsy teasing. His face was stoic, no more phlegmatic than before. The color made her think of heart attacks.

She scanned the alien dashboard with new apprehension. "Can you fly this, Francis?"

"Maybe, maybe not."

She was glad that the engine noise gave her an excuse to yell at him. "Which is it?"

"Which is what?"

She should have been grateful. Being exasperated with him took the edge off her apprehension.

He patted her shoulder. "Yes."

It wasn't much reassurance, knowing that if anything happened to Tommy, her life would depend on Francis the talking fool.

By now, they'd climbed so high, the roads all looked like country lanes. Maxey craned around, ostensibly enjoying the view but actually watching out for other aircraft that Tommy might not have spotted.

She twisted around as far as her seat belt would allow, struck by another question she had to ask. "Do you know my father, Francis?"

"Nope. I've probably seen him drive. I know a lot of drivers without really knowing them, you know?"

It was too difficult to carry on a shouted conversation. Grateful for that, Maxey leaned back to watch Nebraska slide beneath them.

Now and then, the radio sputtered cryptically, mostly numbers. She swallowed, and the engine roared harder.

It was an hour before she realized that the sensation of skimming through the sky, her shadow plowing the empty fields, wasn't all that bad.

7

■ ■ ■

Maxey tensed again when Tommy banked the Cessna and aimed it at the Steamboat Springs airport runway. Surrounded by grassy hills, a single paved strip stretched beside a long, low building the color of peaches going bad.

The motor quieted, the plane floated lower, and before Maxey could do serious damage to the armrest she clutched, they had bumped wheels to the ground and Tommy was braking to a stop. A man in blue coveralls pointed at a row of parked planes, and Tommy idled over to join them.

Maxey let Francis help her out. She walked around in tight circles, loosening muscles and nerves, while Tommy tied down the airplane with quick, sure yanks.

"So how long will we be in Steamboat?" she asked.

"Today and tomorrow. Two nights," Tommy said. "We'll leave first thing Monday, unless they're racing Monday because of rain on Sunday, in which case we'll stay later."

Maxey glanced at the brilliant blue sky, its few clouds as white and insubstantial as smoke. A tourist might have laughed at the possibility of rain, but Maxey knew the Colorado saying to be true: If you don't like the weather, wait five minutes for it to change.

Francis handed her her overnight bag from the storage compartment, and then they trudged into the building. It was the first air terminal Maxey had seen with a massive stone fireplace in the middle of one wall. She pictured it full of dancing flames, surrounded by skiers and their gear.

Tommy told Francis to order a cab, and they had to wait ten minutes in front of the terminal before one arrived. Tommy commandeered the seat beside the driver and the two talked cars the entire trip into town. Francis leaned toward Maxey in the backseat, pointing out sights she might miss, such as Mount Werner looming straight ahead, its ski runs like shaved paths through a gigantic green beard.

"Want to meet for lunch somewhere?" Francis asked her.

"No thanks. I don't want to make any appointments till I've done what I came to do." She congratulated herself for not saying *dates*.

"Sure, but you've gotta eat. Gotta maintain that gorgeous figure. Where are you going to stay, Maxey? You don't have reservations, do you? Everything will be booked solid."

She shrugged, staring out the window on her side.

"You want to share our room at the Sheraton? We can get a rollaway bed."

"No, but thanks."

"There might be a vacancy at a motel on the west side of town," he said doubtfully. "Something either real cheap or real expensive."

A green-and-black-and-white-checkered sign stretched across the highway: VINTAGE AUTO RACE AND CONCOURS D'ELEGANCE. The street was blocked off ahead and people strolled there among antique cars that gleamed and glowed in the sunlight.

The cab jogged right a block, went straight three blocks, jogged left a block, and they were back on the main drag. The Sheraton Hotel hove into view, the gondola ski lift beside it, and tiers of condominiums cluttering the slope below the lift.

"The streets are closed for the racecourse," Francis told Maxey, as if she wouldn't understand why the cabdriver was taking them past the Sheraton and circling around back to it.

As the cab crawled up the hill behind a line of traffic, a faster stream of pedestrians and bicyclists passed them on both sides.

Maxey handed a twenty-dollar bill across Tommy's shoulder. "Apply this to my account," she said, opening the door and more or less falling out, dragging her overnight bag with her. The colorful tide of strangers swept her away. Wherever they were going, it was as good a place as any to begin searching for Deon Burnell.

Except for the orange-slatted safety fence that kept spectators from wandering onto the racecourse, there were no fences. Wherever the line of least resistance had no sidewalk, a path was worn into the grass. People ambled from private property to private property, heading, Maxey hoped, toward the action. The sound of howling motors reminded her of being a child at the entrance to the zoo, hearing the lions roar in their echoing enclosures, wondering if she shouldn't turn back before it was too late.

A multileveled mall of stores and restaurants rose around the entrance to the ski lift. Maxey wanted to stop for a beer, but she was afraid if she shed her overnight bag and sat down, she wouldn't have the willpower to get up and go again. She walked up the open-worked metal steps to the top level and out onto a covered orange bridge spanning a road.

The black bag was a real nuisance. Although not heavy hanging over her shoulder, it took up too much space, bumping against her hip, jostling passersby. She emerged into the scorching sun. Everyone else wore shorts and some kind of hat or cap. The waistband of her tan slacks felt wet enough to wring.

Another bridge led to a path along a hillside of dry waist-high grass. A wire fence kept anyone from falling over the brink onto the highway below, where low, open racers streaked by in some stage of a competition.

Maxey kept walking, past food tents and souvenir stands. She did stop to buy a program from a sweaty boy perched on a high stool under a green-and-purple umbrella. She stepped off the path, between vendors, to skim the pages.

The centerfold was a race schedule: times and groups, makes of cars and their numbers, names of drivers.

Maxey took off her dark glasses, wiped the sweat out of her eyes, put them on again, drew a deep breath of hot, hot air, and began to read down the column of names.

In the near distance, a loudspeaker said, "Look at that driving, folks. He didn't learn that little bob and weave overnight."

Deon wasn't in Group One, Small Bore 2000CC and Under, Class One. She skimmed over into Group Two, Formula Cars, Class One, and down the list of drivers: Aschwege, Staab, Miller, Miller, Rogers, Baum, Burnell.

Maxey lifted the strap of the black bag from the furrow it had dug into her shoulder, set the bag on the ground, and carefully collapsed on it.

Her aunt was right. Her father was alive. Although she'd been shocked to hear it from Janet, seeing his name on a printed page that thousands of others could also see dispelled the niggle of doubt she'd carried all the way from Nebraska.

Now, how would she recognize him? In the few photos she'd seen of him, he'd been young and handsome, flashing white teeth at the camera, his thick blond hair lifting in a breeze, his shoulders square and his waist small. He'd be fifty-something now, going to seed—thicker and thinner in all the wrong places.

She looked at his name again. Next to that was the city and state he came from: Gillette, Wyoming. Damn it, that was just the next goddamned state from Colorado. He'd been in her backyard at least as long as it took to print this information.

"Damn!"

"You okay?" The program boy twisted in his chair to look back at Maxey. His expression indicated curiosity rather than real concern.

She waved him off. Smoothing the program across her knee, she looked at the columns to the left of Deon's name. These, of course, told her exactly how to know him, whatever he might look like now.

Car number: 133. Color: green.

Maxey stretched forward to tug on the tail of the program boy's yellow T-shirt. "How do I get to the paddock area?"

His expression indicated he doubted she'd have the sense to follow any directions he might give. He cocked his head in the direction she'd been walking. "It's right around the corner there."

"Will they let me in?"

"You got twenty bucks?"

She pushed up to her feet and lifted the bag.

"Hey," the kid called as she started away. "No pets allowed. No skateboarding. No liquor. No rap music."

She waved her free hand over her head and kept walking. Around the corner, down a little grade, across a gully. A card table guarded the entrance to the pits. A gaggle of yellow-shirted volunteers accepted Maxey's money, required her signature on a waiver of liability form, and attached a plastic pit pass band to the wrist of her choice.

She squeezed past a knot of tourists, turned to her left, and there she was, at one end of an aisle of bright-colored canopies, trucks, trailers, cars, crews, and drivers. At the far end, the silver metal grandstand rose above everything else, hundreds of human derrieres packed on the risers.

Maxey fell in behind a group of young men sipping soft drinks as they strolled. Curtis and Lance would have loved this.

She didn't expect to find a green car, number 133, right away. When she did, she had to slam on her own brakes and back up several yards to study the layout.

The shiny little car sat empty under a blue canopy on the left side, a third of the way to the grandstand. Feeling a swoop of stage fright, Maxey opened the program to double-check the description. It was supposed to be a 1968 Autodynamics D4B, FV, CC 1385. The only part of this she understood was the date. The little hummer was younger than she and it was designated "vintage."

Three blue-and-white-striped director's chairs were set up beside the car. Behind the chairs, the open tailgate of a pickup truck supported two ice chests and two Safeway bags. The pickup, displaying a Wyoming license plate, needed a wax job on its black paint.

Maxey eased the overnight bag down to the concrete apron in front of her and waited, dry-mouthed. Four men bent over a white car parked in the slot next to the green one, discussing tire pressure. Maxey listened for one of them to call another one Dee.

The loudspeaker overrode their voices. "Group Two, five minutes till grid time."

The black pickup bobbed up and down and a door slammed. Someone circled around from the cab to the tailgate. Of course, Maxey thought. A woman.

But that's all she thought about her before the man came around from the opposite side of the truck. He'd been changing into his red racing suit. Leaving the upper half bunched around his waist, he stopped by the tailgate and rummaged in one of the coolers, his back to Maxey.

He didn't seem tall enough. But all little girls look a long way up at their dads. The rest of his physique matched her memory. His arms could more accurately be called stringy than sinewy, but his belly, when he half-turned and began to drink from the pop can, had stayed impressively flat.

A Colorado Rockies cap hid his hair, or lack of it. The tufts that stuck out through the hole in the back were gray. He started to turn in her direction and Maxey whirled to study the nearest car, a yellow one with a white umbrella stuck in it to shade the driver's seat.

"Would you sign my program?" a high, clear voice asked.

Maxey peeped over her shoulder. A thin little kid in glasses, parents three steps behind him, stood by the green car. The man—*her father*—stretched out a hand to take the program and pen. Maxey picked up her bag and drifted closer.

"Come around after the qualifier and I'll let you sit in the car," Deon said, ending his writing with a flourish. He handed back the program, his smile white in his tanned face.

The boy solemnly nodded before he moved on to the next car and driver. If he could be courageous enough to approach complete strangers, she should have no trouble speaking to her own father.

"Excuse me," she said, holding up her rolled program as if she was trying to hail a cab.

He twisted to look directly into her eyes. When she didn't say anything more, he grinned the dazzling grin. "Hello, darlin'. You want my notorious signature, too?"

He held out his hand and she let him take the program. "Gotta pen?"

"Oh." She dug one out of her slacks. A journalist always has a pen.

"You okay?" he asked, glancing over at her as he wrote. "Sun's a killer today."

Maxey nodded.

The woman had sat in one of the director's chairs. Without looking directly at her, Maxey could have given the police a description. White-blond hair in a ponytail, black shorts and halter, long arms and legs of a shade that could only be called killer copper.

He bobbed his head in a courtly bow as he handed back Maxey's program. He might have scrawled an illegible blur. Instead, he'd printed his name and underlined it with a slash of ink: Deon Burnell.

He shrugged into the sleeves of his red racing suit.

"That must be awfully hot," Maxey said.

"What? The fire suit?" He grinned across at her. "Naw. This isn't

sweat a-dripping off my chin. It's tears of joy to be donning this wonderful Christian Dior creation." He hauled the zipper up and
straightened the collar before glancing at her again. "Something else
I can do for you, honey?"

His husky voice carried a hint of sexual innuendo. Shocked, she
welcomed the rush of anger that restored her to her normal, take-
charge self.

She leaned forward into his face. "How about your address and
phone number? *Honey.*"

He stumbled a step backward, but his grin never faltered. "Hey,
sorry, I'm taken. Tell her, Vonny Jane."

Perfect name. Maxey smiled at the woman sitting by the tailgate
with Deon's white-and-black helmet on her knees.

"If Vonny ever takes off on me, though, I'll let you know," Deon
said, winking at Maxey.

"Dee, look at her," Vonny Jane spoke up. She had a high little-
girl voice that carried clearly above the crowd noise. "Don't you
know who that is?"

Deon, poised to climb into the car, studied Maxey across his
shoulder. She stared back at him, willing him to feel something, a
gene calling to a gene.

Vonny Jane stood up, shielding her eyes against the sun. "You're
his daughter. Aren't you?"

"I don't know. Am I?"

Deon grunted and dropped into the seat of his racer. Methodi-
cally, he fastened the seat belts, lifted the steering wheel off the nose
of the car, and pinned it into position. Arms folded, feet planted,
Maxey watched him think about her.

"You know," he said, reaching for the starter, "you've got god-awful
timing, kid. I'm trying to qualify here. If I wrack up on a turn in the
next few minutes, you can blame yourself for the rest of your life."

"Group Two to the grid," the loudspeaker blared just before the
motor of her father's car drowned it out.

Shaking her head at Maxey, Vonny Jane snatched up a furled umbrella from the truck bed and followed Deon on foot.

Bombarded by the noise of Group Two's engines starting up and moving out, Maxey stood watching the green car nudge its way through pedestrians, around the corner, and out of sight. Then, swinging the black bag into the bed of Deon's truck, she trotted, unencumbered, in the direction he'd driven.

The field was lining up under an orange pedestrian bridge. Deon waited eighth in line, Vonny Jane shading him with the umbrella. Maxey watched from the embankment beside the entrance to the track until whistles blew, signaling crew members to desert their drivers.

Vonny Jane came striding across the road and up into the pit area, straight toward Maxey. "You want to watch from the bleachers?" she called, motioning.

"Sure." Maxey followed her, having to hustle to keep up. Vonny Jane might be as old as forty, but she was fighting it every step of the way. Her legs flexed the muscles of a dedicated jogger, and her buns were tight in the spandex shorts.

They found seats on an upper tier, wedging themselves between two families that hopped up and yelled every time the leading cars came around. Maxey admired the sweeping view of roadways back-dropped by Mount Werner. She wished she had field glasses so she could search for vacancy signs at the motels.

She leaned near Vonny Jane's brown ear. "How did you know who I was?"

"I've been expecting you to turn up someday. And you look like him." Vonny Jane held up one palm to block out the lower half of Maxey's face. "Something about the eyes."

"My cousin thinks I'm the image of my mom."

"Oh, I hope not. I mean, that would be hard on Deon."

"No it wouldn't. He doesn't seem to give a damn about either of us."

"That isn't true."

A trio of racers roared into view, downshifted for the turn, and powered down the hill.

"Give your father a little time to get used to your being here," Vonny Jane shouted into her ear. "Where are you staying?"

"I don't know the name of it," Maxey shouted back in all truthfulness. "Where are you?"

"With friends." Vonny Jane bounced to her feet along with their neighbors on either side as the track announcer called attention to a battle for first position.

Everyone sat down again. After a moment, Deon rushed past the stands, slowed for the turn, gunned away. Maxey thought he must be tenth or eleventh and falling back.

"Is he good at this?" she asked in a lull between cars.

"Not too bad. Usually breaks even. Of course, Steamboat is just for glory. Costs a couple hundred bucks to enter, and there's no prize money."

Maxey ground her teeth together. Her father had deserted her for a dangerous hobby that didn't pay anything.

"How long have you—" A roar of crowd approval for the reappearance of the leaders saved her from finishing the question. Was Vonny Jane his wife? His latest lover? Just a friend who would crew for him?

A psychic, apparently. She grinned at Maxey. "We've been together eight years. I'm engaged and he's just going steady."

In spite of herself, Maxey laughed.

A white-suited official beside the track leaned out to show a blue-and-yellow flag to the oncoming field.

"He'll be hot and tired—cranky as a Model A—when he finishes qualifying. You won't get one decent comment out of him." Vonny Jane laid a hand on Maxey's wrist. "Meet us at the gondola entrance at six-thirty. You know where I mean?"

Maxey nodded, surprised for the help. Now she didn't know what she needed the most—a cold drink, a rest room, or an aspirin.

"See you," she said, slipping out of her seat and away through the crowd.

By the time the last lap was flagged, Maxey had retrieved her bag from the truck and was headed out of the paddock to hunt for room at an inn.

■

"Oh, wow," she muttered. The place was huge, elegant, and all hers for two nights. Never mind that it cost a month's worth of food allowance, just look at that view.

Coming from the pit area, she had stopped at the first building with an OFFICE sign. An elderly gentleman in tennis whites smiled out from behind his counter.

"If you were I, just arrived in town, needed somewhere to stay, where would you try?" she asked him.

"I'd try here," he answered with enthusiasm. "Course, I'd be disappointed when I did. We're full up."

"Give me your expert opinion on where else to ask."

"How much you willing to spend?"

"At the moment, all my worldly possessions."

"I'll call my son up at Chateau Chaminade. Maybe they had a cancellation."

And so here she stood, damp glass of ice water in hand, at the window of a bedroom larger than her own, enjoying the panorama of Steamboat Springs laid out below her. If she tired of this view, she could move to the living room/dining room/kitchen and watch the silver gondolas glide up and down the mountain, a few yards above her roof. All the while, the sound of fast cars whined in the distance, an automotive Muzak.

Maxey opened the double doors to the bathroom, also larger than her bedroom back home, and stripped off her sweaty clothes, debating between a shower massage and a whirlpool bath.

■

Sure that her father wouldn't wait for her if she wasn't there, Maxey arrived at the gondola building fifteen minutes early. Having bought her ticket, she sat on a bench by the big open doorway, watching the ebb and flow of people.

Minutes later, she spotted Vonny Jane and Deon toiling up a slope toward her. They'd both changed into denim blue shirts and jeans. Ponytail swinging with every step, Vonny Jane peered up the hill and waved at Maxey.

"Hi!" Vonny Jane called ahead. "We got so-called free passes to ride the ski lift when we paid our entry fee. So we thought we'd go up on top and have dinner. There's a snack shop up there, you know."

Having reached Maxey, she stopped, hand on heart, to breathe a moment. Eyes fixed dead ahead, Deon marched straight into the gondola barn.

"Come on," Vonny Jane said, waving Maxey ahead of her.

The gondolas paraded in at the back, made a U-turn, and swept out again, in slow, constant motion. A clean-cut young man with enough muscles for the cover of a romance novel monitored arrivals and departures. With nothing real to do in the automated scheme of things, he must have possessed an amazing tolerance for boredom.

Deon strode to a gondola and hopped aboard. Vonny Jane urged Maxey after him with a gentle push to the small of her back. Dropping into the bench opposite her father, riding backward, Maxey slid over to give Vonny Jane plenty of space to jump in.

"Hey!" Deon said, staring out at Vonny Jane, who backed away from the still-open door.

"I'll catch the next one," she said, moving in that direction.

"Christ, Vonny!"

Maxey could see him consider climbing out, but then the door wheezed shut, the cable jerked, and they were launched into the sunlight.

Leaning back, Maxey smiled at Vonny Jane's successful maneuvering. Maxey couldn't help liking the woman who'd given her some very private minutes to spend with her reluctant father. She settled back, prepared to enjoy herself.

"Well, so, how have you been, Dad?"

"Fine." He mirrored her pose, arms crossed. "How about yourself?"

She nodded. "You know that I thought you were dead?"

"Wouldn't make much difference if I was, huh? Kind of a disappointment seeing me in the too, too solid flesh, I expect."

"On the contrary, I'm impressed. That's Shakespeare. The part about the flesh. Do you happen to know Scotty Springer?"

"I don't think so. What's he drive?"

"Never mind. So did you qualify today?"

"For what? World's worst parent?" He unfolded his arms and squirmed up straighter, looking down into the trees.

"Listen, I forgive you. I'm sure there were extenuating circumstances that led you to drop your little girl like a hot radiator cap."

He snorted and continued to examine the scenery. Lifting up the ball cap, he scrubbed at his sweat-damp salt-and-pepper hair. Maxey was glad for him that it still grew thick and low on his forehead.

Vonny Jane's gondola followed along behind them at a constant, respectful distance. Maxey could see her head and shoulders in silhouette against the burning sunset.

Deon craned to inspect the cable as they bumped gently across a support. "Somewhere, I heard you live in Denver?" His inflection made it a question.

"Boulder."

"Married?"

"Not right now."

"Divorced?"

"Yes."

"Well, then, you do know what it's like."

"No kids, though."

"Good. Kids complicate things." He snorted again. "Like right here and now." He reached into his shirt pocket and drew out a pack of Marlboros.

"You can't smoke in here," Maxey said, pointing at the sign on the door.

He knocked a cigarette into his hand. "What are they going to do? Pull this chair over to the side and issue me a ticket?" He jammed the cigarette back into its box and stuffed it all in his pocket again. "You're right. It's stuffy enough in here now."

"Aunt Janet says you killed Mom."

For the first time, he looked at her. His expression reminded Maxey of Reece's the day he admitted he'd cheated on her—regretful, with an underlying terror that she'd begin screaming and foaming at the mouth.

"I've done a lot of disgusting things in my life, but I never killed anybody," Deon said.

"I understand you had an alibi."

"If driving a semi from San Francisco to Albuquerque constitutes an alibi."

"Sounds good to me." She shaded her eyes at the last of the sun. "Is that what you do for a living now? Drive trucks?"

"Yep. Vonny and me both." He laughed and swayed his head. "Can you vision your mother shifting gears and hauling ass along Interstate Seventy?"

"Why do you think Janet thinks you're the murderer?"

"She doesn't think it. She just hates my guts. Accusing me's a way to aggravate my life." He coughed once, a smoker's phlegmy cough.

"Who do you think did it?"

He shifted, planting an ankle on a knee. While she waited for his answer, Maxey felt a surge of hope. Her big, smart daddy would explain it to her, the way he must once have explained about hot stoves and playing in the street. He'd tell her the why and wherefore of her mother's death, and then Maxey could go back to Nebraska and play tourist for the rest of her vacation.

"I don't know," he said. "No idea."

"No," she persisted, "but who do you *think* it was?"

"Damn it, Maxey, didn't I just say I didn't have any idea?"

They stared at one another, and Maxey thought he probably was feeling what she felt—the years falling away, he being the exasperated father and she the pesky, pestering kid. She wanted him to reach out to her—to set her on his lap, give her a hug, or at least pat her face.

Then he looked away, up at the end of the lift, and she chided herself for being a baby.

The gondola hitched up and over the lip of the cliff and scooted inside the shed.

Deon pointed at Maxey. "You stay where you are."

The door popped open and he swung outside. Maxey waited for him to hand her out. Instead, he walked toward Vonny Jane's gondola as it swept forward along the rubber-carpeted dock.

"Maxey's going around again." Deon raised his voice so both women could hear.

Vonny Jane scrambled out, clutching the arm Deon offered her. "You sure you don't want a bite to eat with us?" she called.

Maxey shook her head and moved over into the opposite bench. She felt foolish, gliding around the U-shaped cable like dry cleaning on a rack. The door beside her clamped shut and she rode to the brink of land and out into the sky.

She'd lied when she said she'd forgiven him. She didn't imagine she would ever completely forgive him—especially if he treated her like this.

8

Sunday, race day, sweltered much like the day before. Maxey used a pair of manicure scissors on the pair of jeans she'd brought along, turning them into thready-edged shorts. Having awakened late, she breakfasted on black coffee and a breath mint. Then, unencumbered by luggage, she hiked from condo to pit area—downhill, uphill, downhill.

She found Deon using a long-handled wrench to tighten the lug nuts on his wheels. Vonny Jane had one shapely leg thrown over the arm of her director's chair.

"Hi, Maxey!" she sang out.

"Howdy," Maxey said.

Deon grunted with the effort of his work.

"What's your schedule for today?" Maxey asked him.

"His group practiced at eight-thirty this morning," Vonny Jane answered after a few seconds of Deon's silence. "The race is scheduled for one-thirty, but they're always late getting started."

Deon walked away to the truck.

"We just finished lunch," Vonny Jane said. "Ham and cheese sandwiches out of the cooler. You want one?"

"No thanks. I ate too much last night."

"Where'd you go?"

"Nice Mexican place—expensive, but I'm worth it. Then I went back to the condo and read chamber of commerce pamphlets till lights-out at eleven. You know, a typical Saturday night."

"Come sit in the shade." She patted the seat of the chair next to her.

Settling into it, Maxey knitted her fingers across her fluttery stomach. She didn't blame the latter on last night's chiles rellenos. Her father stirred through a drawer in the red metal cabinet sitting below the truck tailgate, and the tools' angry clatter set her teeth on edge.

"How many different cars have you had since you started driving?" she twisted to ask him brightly.

"Three."

Vonny Jane tipped her head to study her fingernails. She held up the wrist wearing the pits pass bracelet, a strip of neon white against her dark skin. "I hate these things. Make me feel like I'm in the hospital." She stood up. "I'm going over to see a friend in the next aisle. Deon, if you need any help, ask Maxey."

Maxey watched Deon tinker with his car. She thought that if he would talk to her about anything, it would be about his pride and pleasure. But every question she asked met with a terse one-sentence answer. She'd be lucky to get his rank and dog-tag number. He asked nothing of her.

After a while, Vonny Jane returned, obviously disappointed that her leaving father and daughter alone together had not resulted in any significant familial breakthroughs.

"Hi ho, Dee!" a familiar voice hailed.

"Well, if it isn't Tommy Coffman, you old son of a hop toad."

Tommy spread his arms as if to hug Deon, but at the last moment, the two men clasped fists in a hearty grip and patted shoulders with their free hands.

Francis, dressed in a maroon polo shirt, yellow walking shorts, and a white straw cowboy hat, strolled in his father's wake. He cocked his head at Maxey. "You found him, huh? Talked him into making you the sole beneficiary yet?"

"Not funny," Maxey said, aghast at the annoyed glare Deon shot in her direction.

Francis, fanning his neck with his program, wandered closer and dropped into the last vacant chair. He prodded Maxey's upper arm with a sharp forefinger. "Allowing for inflation, two bits for your thoughts."

She realized she ought to introduce him to Vonny Jane, but it seemed too much of an effort, with so very little for Vonny Jane to gain.

"Where should I meet you guys in the morning?" Maxey projected the question in Tommy's direction. "And what time?"

Tommy ignored her, standing wide-legged, hands on hips, in rapt conversation with Deon. Deon shut her out by turning his back to her, keeping his voice low. He laughed a lot.

Francis stretched extravagantly. "Be in the lobby of the Sheraton by, let's say, eight. Sound okay?"

It sounded okay, but it would have sounded a whole lot better if Tommy had said it. Maxey wondered whether any rendezvous Francis suggested would be remembered by him, much less honored by his father.

"Hey, Dad," he now shouted, crossing one bony knee over the other. "How about you and Mr. Burnell taking Maxey and me shopping this evening? If you guys are real good, we'll let you buy us new skis."

Tommy continued to talk to Deon, apparently oblivious, but Deon pinned Maxey with a cold glance that accelerated her stomach discomfort from flutter to flap.

Was this what he thought she was—a female Francis? Did he think she'd searched him out to spend his money, feed on his guilt?

You don't know me. You aren't giving me a chance, she thought.

The loudspeaker called the drivers. Deon shrugged into the top of his suit and lowered himself into the car. Tommy walked beside him, and Vonny Jane strode along behind with the helmet and umbrella as Deon idled through pedestrians, moving toward the grid.

Francis stood and squeezed Maxey's shoulder. "Want to watch from the west fence?"

"No. You go on. I'm going to find someplace to throw up."

Francis laughed and walked away, turning once as if to check that she wasn't really standing on her head in a bucket.

Maxey sat perfectly still, thinking, I got this far without you. I don't need you. You don't know me. Fuck you.

She shoved up out of the chair and headed for the pit entrance.

The pit area was tucked in one side of the hill that the racetrack surrounded. Too keyed up to go straight back to the condo, Maxey followed the fence on a lumpy dirt path worn in the grass overlooking the racetrack. The hill rose steeply on her right, speckled with spectators who had dragged up blankets, cameras and tripods, umbrellas, coolers, and even baby strollers, the better to see the races.

There was nothing to see at the moment. The roadway lay empty and ready. Maxey pictured her father hunkering in number 133, suffering the heat and the noise, and longing for a cigarette, all so he could drive too fast in circles for maybe twenty minutes.

She misstepped on the hard clay, twisted her ankle, and kept on going.

The mutter of engines shifted to a serious scream, and the distant loudspeaker shouted something. After a few minutes, the pack came around the corner, snarling at the heels of the white pace car.

Maxey didn't stop to watch them pass. Still, she couldn't help searching out the green 133 in the middle of traffic, the white helmet sticking up above it like something out of *Star Wars*.

The next time they came around, the pace car had dropped out, and there were already empty stretches between the leaders and the slower cars.

Maxey circled the hill and the track clockwise, the same direction as the racers. Whenever she heard them coming around again, she didn't stop or turn. She wasn't walking up here to see a race; she was walking off a mental cramp.

Deon fell back to about twelfth. For all she knew, this was one of his better days.

She progressed around to the east side of the hill. She could see the orange bridge where she'd have to cross the track. Of course it was covered, so nobody could spit on a driver.

The field had spread out so far by now, the leaders were lapping the stragglers. A swarm of cars went by, there was relative silence, and then a yellow car whipped past, the driver downshifting for a lane change that would funnel him past concrete barricades and under the bridge.

One of his wheels nicked a blue barrel in the lineup to the barricade. It spun him like a bottle cap. Something black flew up and cartwheeled down again.

Maxey grabbed the fence and watched down the track for the next car, its driver oblivious to the danger.

A flash of green—Deon. Of course, her father *would* be the one to come flying toward disaster.

The yellow car had stopped broadside in the lane while the driver tried to get the engine refired. Half of a black tire flopped lazily into the small clear space between the car and the infield wall.

As the green car hurtled toward the yellow one, Maxey's father's life flashed before her eyes. Dead, alive, and really dead, all in a span of three days.

The green car didn't brake. It swayed one way, then the other, in a graceful Z around the tire. The yellow car might have rolled back two inches by the time Deon negotiated the narrows and spurted out the other side.

The little crowd on the hillside cheered. Maxey released the stranglehold she'd clamped on her own throat. She wanted to babble to everyone in range, That's my dad. Is that super driving or what?

All around the track, officials in white coveralls would be waving frantic flags, slowing drivers, probably stopping the race. The yellow car had moved as far to the side as it could go without a tire. The driver was showing a thumbs-up. Somewhere an ambulance warbled.

Maxey stumbled on around the hillside, legs, heart, and lungs pumping.

"He's okay, folks," the loudspeaker crackled. "We're going to call this race over so the crews can clear off number nine turn for the next group."

Maxey kept circling around to the pit area.

A couple of friends were helping Deon run his car into his parking slot. He took off his helmet and blotted his forehead with a sleeve before climbing out of the seat.

Maxey jogged up next to him as he moved to the cab of the truck. "Dad! You were wonderful. You threaded that needle like there was nothing to it!"

He stared at her over his shoulder, his flushed face blank with surprise. "You liked that? It was damned good driving, if I do say so myself."

"I'm glad you're okay."

"Yeah, me, too." He began to peel off the red suit.

Maxey turned around and almost ran into Vonny Jane. She took the older woman's hand and squeezed it.

"Listen, Vonny, I'm really glad to have met you. Thanks for everything you tried to do. Take care of my dad. Don't let him give you any grief."

"You're leaving?"

"Right."

"I know Deon would've liked to take you to dinner tonight, but there's a drivers' banquet—"

"Don't worry about it. Take care. Bye." Flashing a smile so wide that it hurt, she twisted on her heel and walked fast toward the entrance to the pit area.

So that she wouldn't feel as if she was leaving in complete rout, she stopped at the lemonade stand and stood in line for three minutes to buy a two-dollar lemon submerged in a little water and sugar and ice.

Sucking on the straw, she started up the incline beside the fence. "Maxey!"

She half-turned, to find her father striding after her. He'd shed down to a gray T-shirt and gray shorts that matched his gray hairy legs. He kept trying to smile as he approached her.

"Vonny Jane says you're going home now." He stopped a couple of feet away and labored for breath.

"Pretty soon, yeah."

Wiping his mouth with one palm, he stared past her shoulder. "Well, so, it was good seeing you."

"Sure. Good seeing you, too."

His eyes shifted to focus on her face. "You turned out good. Nice-looking and smart. Got a good job, I guess."

She shrugged and smiled. "Right. Good. Everything's good. Not excellent, but good."

"Maxey, I'm sorry—for being such a jerk."

Her lip curled. "You mean twenty-five years ago or now?"

"Both. Mostly now. You scare me, see? I don't like to feel guilty, so I'd just as soon you'd leave me the hell alone."

"I understand." She raised a hand in farewell.

He grabbed it, drawing her forward into an awkward hug. She clung to him, trying not to drip lemonade down his back, feeling like a fool, as strangers swirled around them on both sides.

Breaking the embrace, Deon stepped away. "Did you give Vonny Jane your address and phone number?"

She shook her head, willing herself not to cry.

"Here, write it on here," he said, finding a grocery receipt in his pocket. "Got a pen?"

She nodded, bending far over to write, the tape against her knee.

"Okay, good. Maybe we can get together sometime I'm on my way to Denver or something. Have lunch."

"Could I have yours?"

"What? You want my lunch?" He frowned at her, confused.

"No, you blockhead, your address." She laughed harder than the moment warranted, camouflaging sobs.

"I'll send you a Christmas card," he said. "You can get it from that." He backpedaled several steps, turned around, and loped away.

Oh well, it was a start.

■

She stopped at the mall by the gondola to buy a sack of junk food and a deck of playing cards to hole up with for the rest of the afternoon.

That night, she sat on the sectional sofa with the lights off, watching the unlit gondolas float back and forth across her roof like ghosts that rarely clanked their chains.

■

Monday morning, she packed up, checked out of the Chateau Chaminade, and camped in the Sheraton lobby from 6:00 until the Coffmans came shuffling to the checkout desk at 8:30.

The return flight to Nebraska was pleasantly uneventful. The ride was smooth, Tommy was in a good humor, and Francis asked Maxey for a date only three times. Even the landing didn't seem so bad, though the grass strip was rough enough to rattle them like popcorn.

Maxey had just begun to congratulate herself on a productive trip—she'd found her father and flown round-trip in a small plane without disgracing herself.

Then Francis, who'd just dragged her overnight bag out of the luggage compartment and dropped it on her toes, pointed across the yard. "My gosh, will you look at that? Maxey, look at your car."

Unwillingly, she turned and looked. Her white Ford Escort— *rented* white Ford Escort—had apparently taken part in a demolition derby during her absence.

The three of them walked over to get a better view. A clearer view—it didn't get any better.

"You aren't going to sue us, are you?" Francis asked, circling the car. His father gave him a disgusted look, probably annoyed that he was giving Maxey ideas.

"No, of course not," she hastened to assure Tommy. "It's not anything to do with you."

"Dumb kids," Francis said. "Senseless vandalism. When I was a boy, we'd print 'Wash me' in the dust. Nowadays, they're carving 'Fuck you' in the paint with switchblade knives."

Maxey, who didn't believe for one minute that it was a kid who had snapped off the antenna, kicked dents in all the doors, and stabbed a hole in the rear window, said nothing.

"All the tires look okay. Think they sabotaged the engine?" Francis said cheerfully. "See if she starts up."

Maxey unlocked the door and slipped into the driver's seat, hesitated, thinking of car bombs, and twisted the starter. The motor caught and muttered, ready and willing to go. She was perversely disappointed—now she would have to work up enough courage to drive from this safe, quiet spot to the Witter homestead, exposing herself on the open highway.

Francis unlatched the passenger door and tossed her overnight bag on the seat. "Want to go to a movie next Saturday night?"

Still thinking about the drive home, she almost absentmindedly nodded. "No, I don't think so. I need to spend all my time with Aunt Janet, since I ran out on her this weekend. But thanks."

"Change your mind, anytime," he said, smiling his tooth-heavy smile.

Tommy had already turned away. Too late, Maxey saw him disappear into the house. She scrabbled through her shoulder bag, searching for her wallet. "How much do I owe your dad for airplane fuel?"

Francis waved it off. "He's loaded. He doesn't need it."

"No, that was the agreement. Here. Give him this." She offered two limp twenties out the window.

He took the bills, managing to cover her hand and hold it for a sweaty moment till she inelegantly wriggled it free. As she drove away, she saw him in the rearview mirror, stuffing the money in his back pocket, and she wondered whether Tommy would ever know she'd paid her debt.

All the way to Gruder, she watched for dark pickup trucks full of thugs with knives and hammers.

■

"Well, school starts tomorrow. We could have gone on a picnic if you'd been home the last three days," Janet said with poor grace.

The four of them were finishing supper—fried chicken and all the trimmings—and Maxey had just asked her, "What fun, touristy thing could we do tomorrow?"

"I wouldn't want to go on a picnic anyway," Curtis said around a mouthful of carrot cake. His blond hair needed a shampoo and a trim, and his upper lip bristled with a fledgling mustache. "School or not, I wouldn't go."

His mother set down her coffee cup hard. "What do you mean, wouldn't go? You've outgrown family outings? Too good for—"

"I bet Scotty likes picnics. Don't you, Scotty?" Maxey gushed, hoping to divert the outrage building in Janet's eyes. "Where's the best place to have it?"

Janet scowled. "How about the parking lot of the Highway Patrol? That ought to be safe enough."

Maxey forced a laugh. She wouldn't have mentioned the vandalized Ford if there had been any way to keep her aunt from seeing it out there in the barn lot in all its sorry glory. In the dying light, it looked like a casualty of war.

"Fremont Lakes is nice," Scotty murmured. "Or Pawnee Park."

"You don't have time for picnics, Maxey." Janet wasn't to be sidetracked from a good snit. "You need to go complain to the rental place that they rented you a lemon."

Maxey laughed again, this time genuinely. "There's nothing wrong with the way it drives. They've probably had cars come back looking worse. Like I said, it's insured."

Curtis stumbled up, jarring the table and slopping cups of coffee. "I'm going over to Lance's."

"Don't be too late coming home, because school—"

The back porch screen banged across his mother's demands.

"So you found your dad?" Scotty asked, obviously trying to distract Janet, although choosing the wrong subject for the job.

"I did. We didn't have much time to talk, but we promised to keep in touch now and then." Since Janet's lower lip was already protruding a good quarter of an inch, Maxey sighed and said the rest of what was on her mind. "He couldn't have been in the truck you tangled with Friday, Janet. He was in Steamboat, along with three thousand witnesses."

"He's still got friends here. He could have hired somebody."

"Why? Why on earth would he want to do that?"

"I don't know. Find out why and then you'll find out he's the one did it."

Maxey jumped up to get herself a glass of water she didn't want, counting to ten twice in the process. "How's the clothesline work?" she finally asked.

"Great," Scotty said. "Makes the laundry smell like fresh hay and picks up two extra stations on the TV."

Maxey laughed. Janet's mouth twitched in a grudging smile.

"Great dinner," Maxey said. "I'll do the dishes."

"I'll let you. I'm tired." Janet scraped back her chair and walked away toward the living room. In a moment, a voice exclaimed, "Get two—*two*—great tastes in one" before the TV volume throttled down.

"I'll help you," Scotty said, loading up one arm with a line of dirty plates.

"My apartment has a dishwasher. It's kind of fun, washing dishes the old way like this," Maxey said, twisting on the hot water full blast and plunging both hands into the billowing suds. "For a day or two, anyway."

"Uh, let's see. 'Nothing is really work unless you would rather be doing something else.' James Barrie."

Maxey dropped a handful of clinking silverware into the bubbles. "Has Janet been mad at me all weekend?"

"Don't worry about it. She goes in cycles. Moody as a cat on steroids." He opened a drawer and took out a tea towel. "Good thing she's a superb cook, or I'd have been out of here on the first bus— more than once."

As if summoned by his words, a vehicle hummed up the drive. Leaning toward the window screen, Maxey waited to see what would pull into the barnyard. Then she drew back, her heart performing a little dip and jiggle.

The silhouette of a dark-colored pickup truck loomed in the gray light. It shut off, and no one got out. For a giddy moment, Maxey considered dropping to the floor, out of the line of fire. Then both cab doors flew open and the unmistakable lanky shapes of Curtis and Lance spilled out. They hiked toward the porch, arms swinging and heads down, their voices carrying, the topic being a boss jammer that would blind instant-on radar.

"Is that Richard Chalmers's truck?" Maxey asked Scotty, who stood, towel on forearm, a waiter ready to dry the first dish.

"Affirmative."

"I'd forgotten it was black."

"Like half the other pickups in Dodge County."

The young men clattered into the house and straight up the back stairs, too absorbed in their analysis of how to speed and get away with it to notice Maxey and Scotty.

"What year and make is it?" she asked.

"Chevy. But it's only a couple years old."

"Maybe his last truck was a black Chevy, too. Maybe he always buys Chevys and every one he's bought in the last dozen years was black." Maxey turned around to look Scotty in the eye. He stared back, as expressionless as she.

Maybe Lance had recognized his dad's truck fishtailing out of the driveway just before they found Peggy's body, and maybe that's why he kept avoiding Maxey like she had a world-class communicable disease.

Maxey literally shook off the idea. "Naaah."

"Your auntie's got you as jumpy as she is," Scotty observed.

Maxey scrubbed plates. She couldn't help wondering if her mother had really been involved with a married man, and if that man had been Richard Chalmers.

In less than five minutes, the boys had clattered down the stairs again, jumped into the pickup, and turned it around in a tight gravel-crunching swing on their way to more exciting places.

After Maxey finished scouring the cast-iron skillet and Scotty patted it dry, they were finished.

"Five bucks says Janet's asleep in front of the TV." He hung his soggy towel over the back of a chair.

"Five bucks says you will be, too, before the next station break."

" 'All men are alike when asleep.' Aristotle." Scotty waved Maxey to go in front of him.

"I'm for upstairs," she said, turning in the other direction. "To read in bed. I can't have jet lag. Must be propeller lag."

"Mine's just plain lag," Scotty said, putting one hand in the small of his back and grimacing.

Upstairs, Maxey took her yellow seersucker robe and yellow terry slippers to the bathroom, ran a tubful of warm water, and enjoyed a ten-minute soak. Teeth brushed, freshly shampooed hair slicked back, she opened the bathroom door. A hearty voice floated up the front stairs, inviting everyone to stay tuned for more.

Directly across the twilight-shaded hall was the closed door to the little bedroom that Janet called the junk room. Maxey turned the knob and looked in.

It was aptly named. It looked like the back room of a Goodwill store. A gray-mattressed double bed took up half the space, and the bare springs of another bed leaned against one wall. Three mismatched bookcases held mold-stained books that looked as if the gentlest touch would turn them into mulch. Three china-headed dolls sprawled glassy-eyed on one of the lower shelves. A stack of ornately framed pictures cluttered the bed, mostly painted landscapes, all the colors faded into mud.

Maxey minced her way through a logjam of mildewed cardboard cartons and opened the closet door on a wide but shallow unfinished space. A brass chain hung between bare studs to accommodate cracked leather belts, neckties wide as kites, and one honest-to-gosh feather boa, dusty pink—a very dusty pink.

A long, narrow shelf stretched side to side, eye level to Maxey if she stood on her toes. It was crammed with shirt boxes, hatboxes, shoe boxes, and a tower of music-roll boxes for a player piano. But along the front, except for a stratum of gritty dust, the shelf was empty. The vacant space would have been the perfect size to store a handful of curtain rods.

Maxey stared at the void for a full minute, hearing the television below her feet, smelling mothballs, imagining her mother lifting down the rifle with shaking hands as her life ticked down to implosion.

When Maxey finally tore herself free of the ugly vision, her own hands and knees were quaking like aspen leaves.

9

■ ■ ■

Tuesday's weather was picnic-perfect. Packing a lidded basket with leftover chicken, potato salad, pickled eggs, raw vegetables, and brownies, Janet hummed to herself, her anger apparently in remission.

Careful not to splatter her white camp shirt or white walking shorts, Maxey tasted the lemonade she was mixing, made a face, and reached for the sugar canister again.

"Law," Janet said, holding up an egg as if she'd never seen one stained beet red before. "I never did pay back the eggs I borrowed Friday from Naomi. I'll take her some of these as interest." Janet ripped off a piece of clear food wrap and cocooned three eggs in it. "I'll be right back," she said, opening the refrigerator and yanking out a gray paper carton.

"Let me do it," Maxey said. "I'm ready to go, and you're still in your house slippers."

"Well, all right, but don't let her talk you through the floor. She's a good old soul, but she's lonesome as a leech."

As soon as Maxey began trotting across the grass toward the little gray house due west of the Witter property, she knew she was going to take advantage of this opportunity. Naomi Mercer had been living next door to the Witter family most of her eighty-some years. If anyone knew the gossip about Peggy Witter, it would be Naomi.

Maxey had to make an end run around a wire fence clogged with honeysuckle vines. Watching for poison ivy, she climbed out of the side ditch onto the road and then crossed the ditch again to reach the Mercer yard. A longhaired dog the color of old honey stood on the little front porch to announce her. His bark was strident, but his tail beat the air in great glad sweeps.

Stopping to let him smell her hand, the pungent eggs probably clearing his sensitive sinuses, Maxey called toward the screen door. "Hello, Ms. Mercer? Are you at home?"

The woman who shuffled into view behind the screen was as tiny and thin as a malnourished child. She raised a rusty voice over the dog's commotion.

"Shut up, Elmer." She flapped the door in its jamb, *bang, bang, bang.* "Hah, Elmer!"

When all this failed, she poked two fingers of one hand into her mouth and whistled loudly enough to stop a basketball player in middribble. The dog backed up, sat down, and seemed to smile, tongue draped over his chin.

"Who is it?" Naomi demanded, shading her eyes to look Maxey over.

"I'm Janet's niece, Maxey. Peggy Witter Burnell's daughter."

"Oh."

"Aunt Janet asked me to return the eggs you so kindly let us borrow." Maxey held up the carton and the package of pickled ones.

"Oh. Did I?"

"May I put them in your refrigerator for you?"

"Well, I suppose." She gave the door a halfhearted push and Elmer accepted the invitation, his toenails scrabbling on the hardwood floor inside.

Following him, Maxey found herself in a museum, a musty-smelling high-ceilinged room full of *stuff*—paintings and photographs, figurines, pottery, books, mirrors, baskets, pillows, afghans, dried flowers, lamps, and enough assorted oak and upholstered furniture to fill three rooms the size of this one comfortably. Over everything lay a fur of gray dust.

"Do I know you?" Naomi's face creased with puzzlement on top of age.

"I don't think I've been to your house since I was a little girl."

"The refrigerator's in there." Naomi pointed at an archway. In spite of the heat, she wore a baggy brown sweater over her faded blue dress. Her eyes didn't quite focus on Maxey, as if she had better things to think about. She certainly wasn't the talker that Janet had led Maxey to expect.

"There're pickled eggs, too," Maxey said, trying not to fall over Elmer as he insisted on showing the way.

As she stepped into the kitchen, a man's voice gave the time, and then country violins began to saw. The radio sat on top of a white dome-shaped refrigerator, which rattled quietly to the music. The interior of the refrigerator matched the living room, cluttered and furred. Maxey hoped Janet never borrowed anything that wasn't sealed or boilable.

"I'll put them on the top shelf here."

Shutting the door on the odor of built-up frost, Maxey returned to the living room, eyes front, not wanting to get too good a glimpse at what was hanging out of the wastebasket, encrusting the linoleum, or stopping up the sink.

"How have you been?" Maxey asked, and it was as if she'd shot a starter gun for the most-words-per-minute race.

"I can't complain, but of course I do, though not as much as some, and that's no lie. If it's not my back, it's my bladder, and sometimes both at once, and it's no good seeing a doctor about it, because all they want to do is operate, which is understandable when you think about the overhead they've got—the light and heat and swimming pool and all. So I do what I can with hot-water bottles and baking soda and alcohol inside and out. I'm prit comfortable unless I cough."

On and on it went, a litany, a catalog of bodily dysfunctions. Maxey alternately nodded and shook her head. She wasn't invited to sit. And Naomi didn't sit, weaving instead from foot to foot, a slow dance in time with the cadence of her words.

"Naomi. Naomi?" Maxey finally interrupted, doubting that anything short of rudeness would do the trick. She also doubted that smooth transitions or subtle segues were needed. "Do you remember the day that my mother died?"

Naomi froze in place. "Your mother?"

"Peggy Burnell. Peggy Witter."

"Well, of course. You think I could forget a horrible thing like that? It was sunny, hot. I always suffer with the heat—low blood pressure. The doctor says that low pressure's good and I'll live a long life, but I say what good is living long if you've always got your head between your knees?"

"Naomi, did you see a truck in the driveway about the time Peggy was shot?"

"Certainly. An ambulance. Though of course it was a waste of taxpayers' money to bring an ambulance all the way out here when the poor woman was dead as a wrung-neck hen. I needed the medics worse than she did. I was having diverticulitis so bad, I—"

"Naomi! Any other trucks? Before the ambulance came?"

"Oh, I don't know. Let me think. Seems like I told the sheriff. It was white, too, like the ambulance."

"Are you sure it was white?" Maxey frowned.

Naomi frowned.

Elmer licked up Maxey's shin as if it were an ice cream cone. She pushed him away and he pushed her back.

"Yes, white," Naomi decided. "It had a camper on it, and all the colors of the rainbow on the side."

Maxey saw the light, though she wasn't sure whether it was a beacon or a flash in the pan. "Could it have been a van? The Cloud-Sof van that comes regularly to service Janet's water?"

"Could? Jiggers. It *was*. I think."

"And you mentioned it to the sheriff when he questioned you?"

"Did he question me?"

Maxey's blossoming sense of discovery began to wither toward disappointment. Naomi's credibility might be as dependable as her back and her bladder.

"Did you see anyone that day?" Maxey asked, swatting Elmer's cold nose away from the back of her knee.

"The police—"

"I mean before—who might have killed her."

"I wish I could tell you who," Naomi said, taking the statement as a question. "They shouldn't be running around loose, free to murder some other poor woman."

Maxey couldn't have agreed more.

Naomi raised a trembling hand, about to make a point. "But that white van, now, it might have been some other day I saw it. It's there so much."

"Once a month, I imagine."

"Used to be more."

"It did?"

"That one summer. Not lately."

"The Cloud-Sof van came to Janet's house frequently the summer my mother died?"

"Maybe she washed her hair a lot." Naomi's smile signaled this was a joke. Her eyes lit with awareness for all of five seconds. Then the smile and the intelligence faded away like sunlight behind fog.

"Naomi, did you ever see Peggy with a gentleman friend? Or hear that she had someone that she . . ." Maxey faltered in the search for a euphemism.

"Was screwing around with?" Naomi finished helpfully. "Oh, there was plenty of tittle-tattle, but no names named. Probably just wishful thinking on the part of some nosy old maids of both sexes. Don't you be ashamed about it. Even if it's true, it wasn't your doing. Worrying will only gray your hair and flatten your arches. Worrying is my worst fault. I worry about worrying too much."

"Did Peggy have a woman friend in Gruder? A best friend?"

Naomi considered. "Well, I guess Sophie Dorsey. Sophie Otis, her married name is."

"Does she live in Gruder?"

"Dodge. Her husband's a cardiologist. Whoo, wouldn't that be something, to have a doctor right there in the house all the time?"

Escaping from Elmer and from a graphic account of how worry gave Naomi a stomach virus, Maxey retraced her route toward home. She'd have to get in touch with Sophie Otis to see if she had any ideas about Peggy's murder. Head down, Maxey slowed after she'd navigated the ditch, thinking about Francis Coffman. Why didn't he tell her he knew her mother, if he knew her mother, unless, of course, he didn't want Maxey to know because he'd been Peggy's lover and maybe her killer?

God! Naomi's speech pattern seemed to be contagious.

At the risk of setting off Janet's temper again, Maxey broached the subject as soon as she came in the door. "Hey, did my mother and Francis Coffman know each other? The water-softener guy?"

Janet, who was now completely dressed in a pink pantsuit and thong sandals, looked up from tasting Maxey's lemonade. "They might have had a nodding acquaintance."

"Naomi says she saw the Cloud-Sof van in your driveway a lot during the summer—that summer."

"Naomi probably sees UFOs, chariots of fire, and Elvis on horseback."

"Is there a service-date log on the water softener?"

"If there is, it wouldn't go back ten years, if that's what you're thinking." Janet opened the sugar canister and added another heaping scoop to the lemonade.

"He'd have been—what, thirty? Ten years ago? Would my mother have been attracted to a younger man with above-average teeth and below-average conversational skills? Was he married then? Is he married now? Or maybe his dad was the one—"

"It wasn't Francis or Tommy Coffman who killed your mother." Janet's face threatened to turn as sour as their picnic beverage.

"Okay. I just wanted to check. I'm getting hungry. Is Scotty ready to roll?" Smiling on the outside, Maxey groaned on the inside; she'd have to talk to Francis one more time.

■

It was only a hop, skip, and forty-minute drive to Columbus's Pawnee Park. There were a dozen vehicles parked near the first picnic tables. Maxey counted six dark-colored pickup trucks.

They found a little clearing surrounded by red-berried bushes, remote from anyone else, spread a blanket on the ground for a table-cloth, and enjoyed a leisurely lunch.

Afterward, Janet snapped open a green-and-white lawn chair and settled into it. "This is nice," she said, squirming her bottom deeper into the chair and clasping her fingers across her stomach.

Maxey stretched on her side on the blanket, head propped on her hand. Sunlight dappled by tall sycamores swayed across her legs. "Yes, nice."

Scotty lay in the chair's matching recliner, arm across his eyes, snoring in a slow, steady rhythm.

"We used to come here a lot when I was a kid," Janet went on in a dreamy, storyteller's voice. "My dad would bring his fishing gear, and Mother would bring her crocheting. I liked to explore the paths, pretend I was an Indian maiden. That was before Peggy was born and I had to watch her when we came."

"You were, let's see, fourteen when she was born?"

"Sixteen. Here I thought I was a young woman about to go on dates, make my own decisions, find a young man and leave home. Instead, here's my poor mother, belly out to here, feeling like holy heck, depending on me to be home to cook and clean. And after Peggy was born, Mother didn't feel any better. Cancer had probably already taken root." She died the same year I graduated high school."

"It must have been hard for you, having to be a mother to your little sister."

"I thought so at the time. But she was such a cute little booger, so tiny and blond and quiet. No real trouble to me. It was just that she was always . . . there. I couldn't just pick up and go to a movie or a party or a picnic, the way my friends did. I either had to take Peggy along or find someone to watch her, or, usually, not go."

"I'm sorry, Janet."

"Well, I shouldn't be whining about it now. Like I say, she never gave me a bit of real trouble. She was such a solemn little thing, like she was in church all the time. I dearly loved her. Miss her." Janet leaned over to snatch up her navy canvas shoulder bag and search out a tissue.

"So she grew up and then you felt free to live your own life. You married Harold."

"Yes, and after a bit I realized I'd like to have a little blond girl of my own. But it wasn't in the stars for us. We had a good time trying to have a baby"—Janet glanced over at Scotty, whose breathing rasped in and out—"but nobody ever came of it."

"So you adopted Curtis. And he was an infant?"

"Newborn. Got him through an adoption agency in Lincoln. I'm lucky nobody ever tried to claim him back. You hear of so many heartbreaking stories nowadays."

Maxey nodded.

"He's been a good boy." Janet fingered the ball of Kleenex in her lap. "A *good* boy. I'll miss him, too, when he leaves for the university."

"University of Nebraska?"

"No, Lance Chalmers wants to try Purdue University, so Curtis does, too."

Maxey smiled. "Two peas. That'll make it more expensive for you—out-of-state tuition."

Janet sniffed. "Well, Curtis knows he has to help with part-time jobs. He's signed up for every scholarship we could get wind of, too, so maybe the law of averages will help us out and he'll at least get his books paid for."

"What's Curtis going to major in?"

"Business. And Lance plans on engineering, in case you're thinking Curtis doesn't have any mind of his own."

"No, I think their friendship is wonderful. I wish I had someone that close and special." She rolled onto her back and shut her eyes, wondering if her fireman Calen Taylor would become her best friend. She did find herself missing him.

"Those boys have gone through a lot together." Janet's voice was low and oddly fierce. "They'd either one die for the other."

Maxey's eyes batted open. "Through a lot? Like what?"

"Oh, well, Inez Chalmers's poor health, for one."

Maxey couldn't picture this as something Curtis needed to be much involved in.

Apparently sensing her skepticism, Janet rushed on. "And if you don't think two little boys finding a murdered woman is going to bond them, make them blood brothers for life . . ." Janet flapped her hand, unable to think of a strong finish to the sentence.

A striped squirrel rustled out of a neighboring bush, studied the interlopers for ten seconds, and whisked out of sight again.

Janet blew her nose and cleared her throat. "Where would you like to sightsee tomorrow?"

"I don't know. Whatcha got?"

"We could spend the day in Omaha, at the museums. There's Western Heritage and General Crook and Union Pacific. Have you ever been to St. Cecilia's? That's the most beautiful cathedral. If you like boats, there're the memorials at Freedom Park."

Janet continued to list tourist opportunities, her voice a pleasant buzz against the background of birdcalls and shifting leaves. Maxey fought to stay awake.

"Does that suit you?" Janet asked.

"Mm-hm. Sure."

"And then Thursday we might go to Lincoln and see the capitol. And there's the governor's mansion. They used to have what they called the First Lady doll collection. I wonder if they still do. I wish I still had some of the dolls that I played with. Course, your mother about finished them all off. Literally loved them to death."

"I saw a couple in the junk room," Maxey murmured, half-asleep.

Her aunt's rambling monologue choked to sudden silence. Maxey opened one eye.

"You were in the junk room?"

"Maybe you shouldn't call it junk. Have you seen the prices flea markets charge for—"

"Looking for the rifle, weren't you? I told you I sold it." Janet's voice jangled as effectively as an alarm clock.

Maxey sat up on the blanket. Scotty's snoring broke off and, smacking his lips, he rearranged his legs and opened listless eyes.

"I wasn't looking for the rifle. Just looking," Maxey said. "Is there a photograph album up there somewhere that I could—"

"Why can't you leave it alone? It's done, and nothing will bring her back."

Scotty set a foot on either side of the lounger. "Jannie, let's take a walk."

Ignoring him, Janet leaned toward Maxey, her mouth twisted in an ugly effort not to cry. "You want the truth so bad, next time you see your dad, ask him about the time he tried to rape me."

"Janet," Scotty said, knocking over the chair as he struggled out of it.

"I didn't press charges because I didn't want to hurt Peggy. I don't want to hurt you, either, Maxey, but you're so damned determined to sniff out all the stinking family secrets—"

"Janet." Scotty put his hand on her shoulder.

She shrugged it off. "She asked for it. I want to tell her."

"I'll tell her later. You're too upset. Let's take a walk."

Janet raised her white face to look into Scotty's florid one. "You don't know about the time he—"

"Yes I do. Let's walk." He slid his hand down under her elbow and hauled her up. "Come on, Pocahontas." He winked at Maxey. Still holding Janet as if he expected her to fall or to bolt, Scotty led her into the trees.

Maxey sat on the blanket staring after them, feeling like a bird that had just flown smack into a plate-glass window.

■

"It's a little higher than usual," Scotty said, staring at the river. "We didn't have the flooding around here that they got in Missouri and other places. Except for Crowell. That poor little town is flood-prone. The least little summer shower and Crowell is bailing Elkhorn water."

He and Maxey sat on a flat boulder beside the Loup River. Their closest neighbor was a long-limbed figure in a floppy hat who fished from a canvas chair on a sandbar. Farther downstream, a boisterous family waded in the sluggish brown water.

They'd left a red-eyed Janet at the picnic site, crocheting in high gear, fingers and yarn flying. Scotty wanted to talk to Maxey, make peace all the way around, before they had to shut themselves together in the Bronco for the ride home.

"It's a breakdown in communication is all," Scotty said now.

"She's confused. And there's no point trying to straighten her out. She's going to believe what she wants to believe."

"Where would she get the idea that Deon would . . . do such a thing?" Maxey, whose own eyes felt raw and red, shut them against the sparkle of sun on the water.

"Like I said, poor communication. They happened to be alone in the house. He said something and she interpreted it wrong. Then she probably got into one of her het-ups, tried to slap him maybe. Maybe he grabbed her to make her stop. Maybe he grabbed her in the wrong place. Next, she's yelling, 'Rape,' and believing it. Janet's got a flair for the dramatic. She could turn a dripping faucet into a flash flood."

"When was this supposed to have happened?"

She felt Scotty shrug. "Years ago. When everyone was young and even foolisher than now."

"My father wouldn't murder anyone. He wouldn't rape anyone." She opened her eyes so she could glare at Scotty. "Abandon his wife and daughter—that's the worst he could do."

Scotty reached toward her, drew back his hand. "Permission to pat your hand?"

"Permission granted," she said, bursting into a laugh that verged on tears.

Scotty took her hand and squeezed it. "Your aunt's a pill, sometimes. You've got to swallow her with a grain of salt."

"Okay. Thanks, Scotty."

"Try not to blow on her fire."

"Don't mix your metaphors."

He let go of her fingers and pushed away from the rock.

"Scotty?"

"Well?"

"I'm going to look up my mother's best friend up at Dodge."

He sighed. "Tell Janet you're going to the Laundromat."

"I'm going to the coin laundry," Maxey said airily, a borrowed plastic basket half full of her clothing snugged against one hip.

"You don't have to do that," Janet protested, looking up from the day's mail strewn across the kitchen table. "We can do a load in the wringer washer in the basement."

"No, I don't want to use up your hot water. But maybe I'll bring the clothes home to try out Scotty's new line."

"Well, do you have enough quarters? You know where you're going?"

Janet shouted these last words as Maxey escaped through the back door before her aunt could see that her nose was growing. She hated lying. She would try very hard to make time for both an interview with Sophie Otis and a quick trip to a Suds-Your-Duds.

The wounded Escort limped north from Gruder. Maxey had looked up the Otis address in Janet's Dodge County phone book. Now she spread Scotty's road map on the passenger seat for ready reference. She expected to get lost. She never did in Colorado, but that's because the north-south wall of Rockies rising out of the eastern plain was better than any star to guide by.

She did miss the turnoff from Highway 91 to Dodge, but before she could turn around, there was another one going in the right direction. And the water tower, which looked like a white tin man's hat, did serve as well as any mountain to steer by.

A platoon of portable anhydrous ammonia tanks lined the railroad tracks on the edge of town. Maxey turned onto the main street and cruised the length of it, dutifully looking for a self-service laundry. A gaily colored sandwich sign sat in the center of the brick street: BINGO TONIGHT—AMERICAN LEGION.

She took a cross street at random, sure that she'd intersect Sophie Otis's street sometime, somewhere, without half-trying. A more serious problem was whether Sophie would be at home. Maxey hadn't called, not wanting Janet to overhear the conversation. Since Dodge was an easy drive from Gruder, Maxey preferred to try again another day, if need be.

Need did not have to be. Sophie's pale blue two-story house bore a big brass identification number, and a lady of about the right age knelt under a tree in front of it. Hopes high, Maxey parked the Ford and got out in a hurry, before her quarry could disappear.

10

∎ ∎ ∎

"Hello," Maxey called, sliding her dark glasses to rest on her hair. "I'm looking for Sophie Otis."

Hands full of ousted dandelions, the woman stared up at her. "Don't I know you?"

"I'm—"

"No, don't tell me. Let me think." She shut her eyes and dropped one handful of weeds to pinch the bridge of her nose. After a full minute, Maxey was afraid she'd gone to sleep.

"You're"—the woman looked up in triumph—"Penny Overholtzer's daughter."

Maxey's encouraging smile died. "No. Close, though." She had no idea who Penny Overholtzer might be.

"Wait! Hold that look. Don't smile. You're—oh my God, you're poor Peggy's daughter."

"Right. You're her friend Sophie."

"Oh my. They used to call us 'Yin' and 'Yang' because she was so quiet and I was so not quiet. Let's see, your name is Marcie."

"Maxey."

"And you live in Colorado."

Maxey nodded. One out of three wasn't too bad. "I'm visiting my mother's sister for a week—Janet."

Sophie nodded, grinning as if she'd just unwrapped a wonderful present. She had a wholesome look about her—blond hair in pigtails, a tan and freckled face, a fit little figure in jeans and a short-sleeved white shirt. The kind of woman who would jog two mornings a week and golf most of the rest. Surely Maxey had met her—at the funeral, if not before—but no recollection of it surfaced.

Sophie dropped the dandelions into a spread newspaper, rolled it up, and stood effortlessly. "Let's have some iced tea."

Maxey followed her around the house to a sunny flagstone patio surrounded by flower beds and bushes. Depositing the newspaper in a trash can artfully hidden in a triangle of hedge, Sophie motioned at a round white table covered by a pink-and-white-striped umbrella.

"Have a chair. I'll be right back."

With her face in the shade and her legs stretched into the sun, Maxey folded her arms and listened to the birds. A few doors down, someone shouted for Dopey to come home. Or maybe it was Toby.

Sophie bustled down the shallow porch steps with two tall, clear glasses of tea and ice cubes. "I'm so glad to see you. If I'd known you were coming, I'd have made a coffee cake to go with this."

"I didn't call you because I didn't want you to go to any trouble. And I won't stay long. I just wanted to talk about my mother some."

The tea was full of sugar and lemon. Why did people always ask how a guest liked her coffee and never ask how she liked her tea?

"You talk about Peggy all you want, Maxey. I'm a good listener."

"No, I mean, I wanted to hear about her. I've been feeling sort of guilty that I didn't know her better—that I didn't know what was going on in her life. Right before she died, especially."

"Oh. Okay. What do you want to know? Not that I'll know either, you understand. Peggy was a very private person. She'd have been perfectly happy to have gone to Innisfree and lived alone in Yeats's 'bee-loud glade.' "

Maxey paused, glass below her mouth. "Do you know Scotty Springer?"

Sophie cocked her head to one side. "I don't think so. Should I?"

"He likes quotations, too. He's Aunt Janet's gentleman friend."

"Oh, uh-huh."

"Did my mother have a gentleman friend? Just before she died, I mean."

Sophie propped her chin on her fist and considered. "No."

"Are you sure? The sheriff seemed to think she did, and that he might have killed her."

"Oh, the sheriff." Sophie flapped one hand in dismissal. "He was grasping at straw men. Your mother never much liked sex. Or men in general, for that matter. She would have told me if she'd changed her mind about it. She didn't."

Maxey swallowed tea and a little bit of pride. "Did she love my dad?"

"She thought she did. When we graduated from high school, the going thing for females was to marry and have babies, preferably in that order. Today, she could have built herself a nice career instead—run a bookshop or something."

"I guess that helps explain why Deon left."

"I'm sure it wasn't easy being married to someone with as much generalized dissatisfaction as your mother had. She didn't know *what* she wanted; she only knew she wanted *more.*"

Maxey felt a sudden useless wash of guilt that *she* had not been what her mother needed. They should have talked more often. Maxey should have put the same effort into cheering her mother as she did in escaping from her and from home.

"So what's your theory, Sophie? Who killed her and why?"

Maxey waited through the long, thoughtful silence that preceded Sophie's answer. A honeybee zipped under the umbrella on its way to the floral smorgasbord beyond. In the middistance, an infant's wail climbed and stilled.

"She knew something someone didn't want her to know," Sophie said. "She saw or heard something."

Maxey set down her glass too hard. "Did she tell you that?"

Sophie laughed. "If she did, wouldn't I be dead, too?"

"Then what makes you think—"

"What other explanation could there be? It wasn't a botched robbery, because nothing was stolen, not even the rifle. No one would have murdered her out of jealousy or revenge or rage, because she was too colorless to inspire any of those. She didn't have an estate that her greedy heir would murder her to get. What's left?"

"A random crazy?"

"It's possible, but there weren't any other unsolved murders in the area before or since. My gut feeling is, she must have discovered something volatile, and it led to her shooting."

"You don't think she was blackmailing someone!"

Sophie didn't have to think about it. "Of course not. She didn't have the imagination for that."

"Don't be offended, but I have trouble picturing you wanting to be my mother's best friend. You are so outgoing—so yang, as you say, to her yin."

Maxey held her breath, half-expecting Sophie to reveal that Peggy and she had been lesbian lovers.

"She saved my life once. That kind of thing tends to dispose you favorably toward the savior, no matter how morose her personality."

"No kidding," Maxey said, still startled by the saved-life part. "How'd she do that?"

"We were just kids, seven or eight maybe. Our school had this stupid rule that if you lived within a mile, you couldn't ride the school bus. Since the school was on the south side, all of us from the north and west edges of town had almost a mile to walk. They also wouldn't let us eat in the cafeteria, but that's another story." Sophie squirmed back into her chair, warming to the narrative.

"Of course that meant we had to cross the railroad track at least twice a day. Even the little first graders, which makes me shudder to think of today."

"Anyone home?" a male voice called from the depths of the house.

"Out here, sweetheart," Sophie shouted, her face brightening with expectation.

A white-haired man in a light gray suit and bright yellow shirt, his mostly blue tie loose at the collar, trotted gracefully down the back steps. Kissing the top of Sophie's head, he openly studied Maxey. "Company?"

"Maxey, this is my husband, Dennis. Maxey is Peggy Burnell's daughter."

Maxey reached across the table to shake his hand. His expression befitted a doctor with a bedside manner. His brow wrinkled in pained concern. "It gripes me all to hell that no one's ever been arrested for what happened to her. Sophie misses her."

Maxey smiled and nodded.

"Have you seen my golf shoes, Soph?"

"The utility room."

"Thanks. Nice to meet you, Maxey."

Maxey smiled and nodded, feeling like a lump. He had Paul Newman eyes. If his patients didn't have heart palpitations before they came to see him, the more susceptible females must surely have them after.

As the screen door slammed behind him, Sophie stretched and rearranged her legs. "His office is in Fremont, close to Memorial Hospital. This is his afternoon off, so of course he's playing golf. Did you ever hear of a doctor who likes to bowl? Why not, do you suppose?"

"You were telling me about what happened when you were a girl," Maxey said.

"Oh, yes." Sophie took a moment to gather herself, staring into the distance and the past. "I'd been to the movies. I think it was *How Green Was My Valley.* Or maybe *The Boy with Green Hair.* Anyway, there was a truly disturbing part in it where a boy's foot got caught in a railroad track. He was running across the tracks and a siding switched, and so there he was, trapped. And, of course, a train was coming. The scene was shot from the perspective of the doomed boy. It was horrible to hear the whistle and see the light and then the gigantic engine bearing down on you. It was one of those big black steam engines like's parked at the entrance of Pawnee Park. Do you want some more tea, Maxey?"

"No thanks. I'm fine."

"Well, so there I was one sunny afternoon after school, approaching the Gruder tracks. The teacher had kept me a few minutes late to give me an assignment I'd missed, and my friends were all about a block ahead. Even though I could see the red warning light start to blink, I didn't want to wait for the train, because then I'd have to walk all the way home by myself. I thought I could beat it if I ran. And I really could have, except when I was halfway across, I made the mistake of looking down the track at the train. And then I was stuck, as surely as that movie boy, panic-stricken, mesmerized by the monster that was bearing down on me." Sophie hugged herself against the memory.

"While I took root there between the rails, Peggy came running up the street behind me. She was screaming for me to look out— as if I couldn't see the damned train. When she realized screaming wasn't enough, she came roaring after me herself. She had sense enough not to push me. We'd probably both have fallen forward and been killed. Instead, she grabbed my arm hard enough to leave bruises for a week, yanked me backward off the tracks, and we rolled into the side ditch. Then we held each other in a hammer-lock and had hysterics while the freight rattled and boomed two yards above us."

"She never told me," Maxey murmured.

"She never told anyone. I made her promise never to tell anyone. I was mortified at how dumb I was—trying to outrun a train and then not running! Here, this is clean."

Maxey patted at her eyes with the proffered tissue from Sophie's shirt pocket. "My mother, the heroine."

"Yes. And here I am, breaking my own vow not to tell. She would never have blabbed. Whatever the secret is that she was killed for, she would never have revealed that, either. Her murderer shot her for nothing."

The sound of a starting lawn mower bit into the afternoon quiet. It was far enough away to be a whine instead of a scream.

"Peggy and I had scarcely exchanged three words to each other before that day," Sophie said. "If she hadn't done what she did, I'd no doubt have gone on blithely ignoring her, hanging out with my little clique. Little Miss Snob and the Snobettes. Come to think of it, she saved my life twice!"

Maxey sighed. "Thanks, Sophie. You've given me a lot to think about."

The women stood and shared a fierce embrace, Maxey thinking, *This hug's for you, Mom.*

"Is there anything else I can do for you?" Sophie asked.

"Could I have another glass of tea after all? Without sugar or lemon?"

■

"Scotty and I will do the dishes," Maxey said, putting her napkin beside her empty bread-pudding dish.

"Whoa, wait a minute, before you spoil Janet for me," Scotty protested. "I've got to live with her after you go home."

"Do you eat this high every day when I'm not here? Does Janet always feed you meat and potatoes?"

"No, now that you mention it."

"See. Maybe if you did the dishes—"

"Something to think about," Janet said, tidying up Curtis's place at the table.

Curtis had excused himself before the rest of them were half through the meal, carrying his dessert bowl with him as he rushed out toward the perky beeps of a car horn. Lance was driving the cute little red convertible instead of the big black truck.

"I'll wash; you dry," Scotty said to Maxey.

Janet stood in the middle of the kitchen, looking lost for a moment. "When you get to the pots and pans, give me a holler. They're so mean to do." She wandered in the direction of the living room.

"As if we don't have enough smarts to scour pots and pans," Scotty said, squirting dish detergent with a flourish.

When happy commercial music sounded from the front room, Scotty glanced over his shoulder at Maxey. "I saw your undies hanging on the line out back, so I deduce you hunted up your mother's friend today."

"I did. And I'm glad. She told me some nice stories about my mother. She says the speculation about a mystery lover was all baloney. Mother didn't tell Sophie about him; ergo, he didn't exist."

"Does that make you feel better or worse?"

Maxey frowned at the dinner plate she was drying. She could see herself in it. "Do you happen to know her husband, Dr. Dennis Otis? In person or by reputation?"

"Can't say I do. What kind of doctor is he?"

"Heart."

"There you go. I'm all heart, and it's in perfect health."

"He's a good-looking dude. I feel terrible about being so suspicious, but I can't help thinking that if my mother did have a lover, she wouldn't have told Mrs. Otis if the man was Dr. Otis."

"And he killed Peggy to keep his wife from finding out?" He sounded decidedly skeptical.

"Don't you think it's possible?"

"Does Sophie Otis have a better theory?"

"She thinks my mother stumbled on information that threatened the killer in some way."

Nodding, Scotty loaded the first saucepan into the wash water. Sweat trickled down his face to the thicket of chin whiskers, and Maxey ripped off a paper towel from the dispenser to pat his forehead.

"Secrets, bah humbug," she said. "Give me a quotation on the topic of secrets."

"Hmm. Well, I've heard that you should tell your friend a lie, and if he doesn't spread that around, you can safely tell him a secret."

"Seems like sound advice to me." Maxey took the rinsed pan and began to dry it.

"Oh, and Benjamin Franklin had a good one. Let's see. 'Three may keep a secret—if two of them are dead.' "

"That *is* a good one. You can't beat old Ben when it comes to cracking wise. Oops, you didn't have enough smarts to get all the mashed-potato muck out of this pan."

"Leave it. It'll gratify Jannie no end."

■

On Wednesday, with Scotty doing all the driving and Janet rattling off a tour-guide spiel, Maxey inspected Omaha, the Crossroads of the Nation.

Since she had expressed an interest in historic buildings, they cruised past the Civic Auditorium, the Orpheum Theater, Rosenblatt Stadium, the Bank of Florence. They spent an hour strolling through St. Cecilia's Cathedral. For lunch, they parked and staked out a sidewalk table at an Italian restaurant in the Old Market Area. After they'd demolished an extra-large ham and pineapple pizza, Scotty proclaimed the meal good but the fellowship even better.

Given her druthers, Maxey chose the zoo for the rest of their afternoon. Walking through the tropical rain forest, smelling sweet vegetation and musk, hearing shrieks from unidentifiable beaks, feeling humidity seep into her skin, she felt more at peace with herself and the world than she'd felt in weeks. A tiny brilliantly turquoise bird skimmed to rest on a deep green leaf overhanging the path, and she amended *weeks* to *years*.

"I'm going to buy a membership in the Denver Zoo," she announced, swiveling toward Janet and Scotty, who walked arm in arm behind.

Janet smiled, brightly and too late. She'd worn a different expression when Maxey surprised her, one that reminded Maxey of the way Janet had looked at the glassed-in snakes. For several minutes afterward, Maxey thought about that look, until she convinced herself her aunt's sour face had been a stomach cramp or a headache twinge and nothing to do with her.

■

They arrived home at about five o'clock, too tired and hot to eat supper.

"Every man for himself," Scotty declared. "I'll just fix myself a bowl of cereal—after my nap." He walked purposefully toward the living room and the couch.

Curtis had left a note magnetized to the refrigerator: "Jody asked Lance and I to supper tonight."

Janet shook her head. "Look at that grammar. And he's to graduate in nine months."

"Who's Jody?" Maxey asked.

"Lance's girlfriend, Jody Hellman. Did you know any of the Hellmans who had the bakery in town?"

Maxey shook her head.

"Well, of course you didn't. I keep forgetting you never lived here. I forget you aren't Peggy." Janet opened the refrigerator and began foraging for leftovers.

"Does Curtis have a girlfriend?"

"Oh, yes. Girlfriends, plural. But that's all they are—just friends. Thank goodness. We may actually make it out of the teenage zone without hitting any of the major potholes—drugs, pregnancies, or DUIs. Here's enough roast beef for a sandwich. Or would you rather have chicken?"

"Got any peanut butter?"

The telephone at the end of the counter jangled.

"Want me to get that?" Maxey asked, already on her way. "Hello?"

"You're just the lady I wanted. Take that any way you want, ha-ha."

"Who is this?" Maxey's tone of voice made Janet back out of the refrigerator and turn to stare.

"Who do you think it is?"

She still didn't recognize the voice, but she recognized the style. "Francis."

"Bloody well right." He breathed, waiting. It was her turn, after all.

She smiled, imagining how surprised he would be. "You're just the man I wanted to talk to, too. How about meeting me somewhere for a drink?"

"Sure," he said with maddening lack of surprise in his voice. "Name a time and place."

"Tonight, but you'll have to say where, since I'm not familiar—"

"Nope, I can't make it tonight. How about tomorrow?"

"Okay. About seven-thirty?"

"Let's make it The Alley, eight o'clock. Whoa-ho, Maxey, have I got something to give you!"

"The alley?"

"Wear something blue. You look smarmy in blue. Ta."

Fuming, Maxey replaced the phone. "Is there a tavern around here called The Alley?"

Janet paused in unwinding a shroud of clear wrap from a head of lettuce. "In West Point. It's a bowling alley."

Maxey groaned. "The perfect place for a talk."

"I thought you didn't like Francis."

"I don't. Come to think of it, I guess I should be grateful it isn't a candlelit restaurant with canned violins playing Elton John songs."

"If you don't like him, why meet him anywhere whatsoever?"

"I'm using him."

Baffled, Janet went back to making herself a sandwich. "Seems like you should use someone you might enjoy recycling someday."

Laughing, Maxey reached for the instant coffee. She pictured Reece waiting for her at her curb, his hairy arms and legs dangling out of a green plastic recycle bin. No, that was the wrong image. She was the used and Reece was the user.

A surge of worry hit her. "What's today? Wednesday. Oh God. I hope Reece had the newspaper ready to send to the printer this afternoon. Maybe I should phone him. But what good would that do? I couldn't do anything about it from here."

Janet wasn't listening. "Now about tomorrow. Do you have your heart set on going down to Lincoln? Because if you don't, I'd like to suggest we go shopping." Janet lowered her voice and swayed closer to Maxey. "Scotty's birthday is Friday, and I haven't idea one what to get him."

"Sure. I love to shop."

"Well, so of course we can't have Scotty along. Would you care if I invite Inez to go with us? She doesn't go and do very often unless I pester her into it."

"That's a nice idea. Give her a call."

The women sat down at the kitchen table with hot coffee and cold sandwiches and began to eat without much interest. Maxey decided not to think about Reece. After all, if he did nose-dive the paper into the ground while she was gone, she wouldn't have to worry about Clark Dumpty being her business partner.

■

"Did you tell Scotty why he couldn't come along?" Maxey asked Janet as they tooled south out of Gruder on their way to pick up Inez Chalmers.

"I didn't have to. He knows when his birthday is." Janet pulled the rearview mirror sideways and spent a long time studying her lipstick in it. It made Maxey squirm a bit, since Janet was driving.

"Did you ever decide what was wrong with your car?" Maxey asked, watching out the windshield for a reason to grab the steering wheel.

"Wrong with my car? Oh, I think I flooded it is all. Naturally, it started on the first try for Scotty." She returned the mirror to its proper position. "I'd forgotten about it. I hope it doesn't give us any trouble today. Maybe we should have taken your rental, just in case. Although I'd hate to be seen in such a junk heap."

The east-west roads below Gruder had letters for names. Janet turned on J and they continued a few miles more before she slowed for another turn into a lane.

Maxey had pictured the Chalmers family living in a cozy Victorian farmhouse similar to Janet's. Instead, the house rose out of the cornfields like a glass and stone whale, all rounded corners and shades of gray. Four maple trees formed towering parentheses on either side of the entrance to the gravel driveway. Formal flower beds, the chrysanthemums as colorful as fireworks, bordered the drive to the attached three-car garage. Twin stone lions kept vigil on either side of the white concrete path approaching the navy door.

Before the car rolled to a stop and Maxey could offer to get out and go ring the doorbell, Janet pushed two long bleats on the horn, and Inez came hurrying out. Maxey moved to the backseat, holding the door for Inez in the process.

"Now, this is going to be fun," Inez said, struggling to fasten her seat belt. "Who are we going to buy out first?"

"Is Crossroads Mall okay with everybody?"

Inez chirped agreement, and Maxey, a stranger in a strange land, said, "Yes, of course."

"You have a beautiful house, Inez." Maxey twisted around to read a black and brass sign atop the country mailbox: RICHARD C. CHALMERS, CERTIFIED PUBLIC ACCOUNTANT.

"Inez always keeps it at its best, in case *Better Homes & Gardens* should call," Janet said. "You can see your face in her sidewalk."

"Are you enjoying your visit, Maxey?"

"Sure. I'll pay for it when I get home, though. Having to diet off the pounds I gained on Janet's yummy cooking."

"Inez, did you see that doctor in Schuyler you were talking about?"

"Tuesday."

After a moment's silence, Janet prompted, "And?"

"Well, he did some tests, and I haven't heard back yet."

"Did he say anything good or bad?"

"No. Come on, don't let's talk about me and spoil the morning. Did you know that Billie Murray had her baby? A girl this time."

"Oh Lord. I'll send her a sympathy card. What does this make—ten potential felons?"

"Eleven, if you count her husband, Leroy."

As they drove toward Omaha, the two ladies discussed people and events that Maxey didn't know or want to know about. Lulled by miles of cornfields and ubiquitous railroad tracks unrolling outside her window, she tried to keep her eyes open and her head upright.

"There must be more grain bins than houses," she said once, but she didn't get any response from the front seat, where the topic of the moment was Jody Hellman's father's sister's gallbladder.

Giving up, she jammed her shoulder bag against the window and her head against the shoulder bag and slept.

■

At the mall, they parked, took a bearing, and entered by way of Sears. The smell of new merchandise was as heady as good perfume. Janet set a course for the men's clothing department, stopping at every ladies' wear rack en route.

"I could use a new ironing-board cover," Inez said, rising on her toes, as if the extra inch would help her see into the housewares area.

Maxey drifted in their wake, content, her worries submerged by the siren surfeit of consumer goods.

A card table sat double-parked next to a jewelry case. It held a glossy white-and-red sign: FREE!!! CELLULAR PHONE FREE!!!

The clean-cut young man sitting beside the table smiled at their approach as if this was everyone's lucky day. "Good morning. Wouldn't you ladies like a free telephone?"

"What's wrong with it?" Janet asked.

"Absolutely nothing. It's thirty-two digital, eleven alpha character capacity, alpha memory and scan, ninety-nine phone number memory, with a four-and-a-half retractable antenna."

"No wonder you're giving it away. Who could figure out how to use all that?"

"Ha-ha. You could. And there's more. Call tracking, dual NAM, SID. . . ."

"This boy's overqualified," Inez murmured to Maxey. "He'll never sell his free phones if he doesn't talk down to us electronics illiterates."

They sidled politely past the table, the salesman talking faster as he saw he was losing them. "An optional three-watt vehicle booster kit, and for a limited time only, one hundred minutes of free talk time. Just think how many blouses and skirts you could buy for that."

Janet stopped walking. "How many?"

"Fifty dollars' worth."

"He hasn't checked the price of women's clothes lately," Inez said.

"Yes, but one good new outfit is all I need," Janet said.

Maxey was about to laugh until she saw her aunt lean down, frowning, to examine the sample phone.

"This works in the car?"

"Yes, ma'am. Or in your office, your house, anywhere. We give you the unit, and then you pay just thirty-two ninety-five a month. That's only about a dollar a day, plus about fifty cents per call. Your first ten calls are free."

"I bet Scotty would like one of these." She looked at her companions, both of whom shrugged.

"It's a three-hundred-dollar value," the man coaxed.

"Where else can I get him a free birthday present worth that much?"

"It won't be free when he starts using it," Maxey said.

Janet flapped a hand in dismissal. "That's okay. He can afford the forty dollars a month. I'll take one. I don't suppose you gift wrap?"

■

Their arms full of crackling plastic bags, Janet and Maxey managed to open the back door and straggle into the kitchen.

"What time is it?" Maxey asked, twisting to see the clock over the stove. "Six-ten? How'd it get so late! I'm going to have to hustle to get ready for my big date at the bowling alley."

Janet yanked a sticky note off the refrigerator door. "Scotty and Curtis went to get a part for Curtis's car. Good. That gives me a chance to put away Scotty's present and my guilty pleasures undetected." She took a tighter grip on the packages and headed for the back stairs.

Maxey followed, debating with herself on whether to take a quick shower. She would come home from The Alley smelling of cigarette smoke anyway, so she might as well wait. Of course, if her assignation were with Mel Gibson, there was no question she'd take a shower, manicure her nails, and shave under her arms. Francis Coffman was lucky if she took time to brush her teeth.

"Okay if I use the bathroom first?" she called to Janet, who had just turned the corner into her bedroom.

"Go ahead. Will you want something to eat?"

"No. I'll pick up a sandwich at The Alley."

"That sounds disgusting."

"It probably will be."

Maxey dumped her day's purchases on the bed—four pairs of plain white panties and one pair of plain white athletic shoes for her and a big colorful book called *History Through Maps* and a sheet of psychedelic paper to wrap it in for Scotty.

She hunted her cosmetics bag out of the shoulder bag and carried it to the bathroom. She'd save the shower for tonight.

Having used and flushed the toilet, she washed her hands at the pitted sink. The taps were the old-fashioned kind—one for hot and a separate one for cold. The hot always started out cold and then it ran too hot to touch. There was a window of opportunity between the two temperatures when, three bears–style, it was just right. Maxey smeared Noxzema on her face, waiting for that moment.

Judging it to be about now, she bent forward to rinse her face with her cupped hands. Just before she shut her eyes, she saw something that jerked her backward, making her bang her elbow on the edge of the sink. She stared, her hands still raised and ready.

The water that came splashing from the spigot and went swirling down the drain had turned red.

11

. . .

Maxey made herself reach out and shut off the faucet. She turned on the cold and watched it run clear for several seconds. The sink, where the hot water had drained away, was stained a sickly pale red. Maxey touched it tentatively and brought the finger up to her nose to smell it. Nothing. She was too chicken, or too smart, to touch it to her tongue.

She opened the hot tap and watched the red dance out again. Like strawberry Kool-Aid, or very thin blood.

Closing it down to a trickle, she cleared her throat, opened the door, and called her aunt.

"What?" came the muffled answer, probably from Janet's closet.

"Could you come here a minute?"

In a moment, Janet arrived, carrying an empty sack she folded as she came. "What's wrong?"

"Has this ever happened before?" Maxey stepped back and motioned at the sink.

"Oh my gosh, Maxey, did you cut yourself?"

"No, no, I'm fine. The water started running red out of the faucet."

"It did what?"

Since Janet could see for herself as much as Maxey could tell her, Maxey didn't reply. Janet dropped the sack and clutched the sides of her face. They stared at the sink and tried to think of an explanation.

"The house is haunted," Janet finally said. "They'll make us into a movie."

Maxey lifted the lid of the toilet and confirmed that it was full of colorless water. "Only the hot water seems to be affected."

Janet held up one index finger. "Must be the water softener's gone berserk, then. But scarlet, for goodness sake?"

They trooped down the stairs and into the utility room behind the porch. The water heater, trying to replace the pint or so that Maxey had used, rumbled busily. In front of it sat two round cylinders labeled CLOUD-SOF. Janet pried up the lid of the larger one, and both women swayed forward to peer inside.

"What in the world . . ." Janet's voice quivered and faded away.

On top of the white salt pellets that nearly filled the container lay a sheet of yellow tablet paper. The printing was in black marker, smeared by moisture: "This time die. Next time maybe cyanide." The lower half of the container was spattered and stained like an abattoir.

Maxey's first thought concerned the kittens.

Janet groaned and rocked from foot to foot, breathing as if it hurt.

Maxey picked up a broom and used the handle to stir the salt pellets out of the way. "It's not as bad as it looks," she said. "Whoever wrote the note misspelled *dye*. The bottom's full of food-coloring bottles. Someone must have emptied all the area groceries of red dye number whatever, then poured all the bottles into this tank."

"I've got to sit down," Janet mumbled, and shuffled toward the kitchen.

Maxey left the broom sticking out of the mess and followed her aunt, who walked all the way into the living room and collapsed on the couch, one foot on the floor, one arm over her eyes.

"Enough to give a person a heart attack," she muttered.

Maxey patted her on the knee before taking a chair across the room. "How does the water-softening system work?"

"Francis Coffman brings the salt once a month and loads the softener. Then every now and then, some of the mixture dumps into the water heater, I guess."

Maxey found a tissue in her skirt pocket and wiped the Noxzema off her face. "So anything in the softener tank would get added to the hot-water supply?"

"I guess." Janet took the arm away from her face. "Cyanide, for instance. Well, as soon as Scotty gets home, he's disconnecting the damn thing." She hugged herself and gazed at the ceiling, her face slowly losing its library-paste complexion. "The gall of someone, coming in my house while we're all out shopping. What we should have bought was padlocks and another rifle."

■

"It didn't have to be this afternoon, you know," Francis said. "The dye could have been added to the tank anytime in the last week since I was there. I could have put it in when I was there." He grinned his superior toothy grin and waited for Maxey to react.

They sat on opposite sides of a booth that overlooked the bowling lanes, mercifully behind a wall of semisoundproof glass. Maxey had half-expected him to be bowling on a league team, with only a few moments to spare her between spares. However, he'd chosen The Alley for its excellence in hamburgers, he said. The cook was still perfecting their order while they drank lite beers and munched potato sticks.

"I saw a timer," Maxey said. "You or the customer can set it to release the salt solution anytime you want."

"Is that what you think?"

Maxey clenched her teeth to hold in harsh words. The evening was young and she still had a lot of questions to ask the big twit.

"Please," she said sweetly. "Explain it to me."

"You're right about the timer. A lot of folks set it for the middle of the night so they don't have to hear it run. Sounds like a tub spilling over." He settled back, one arm along the back of the bench, the confident expert in his field. "The new timers are electronic, but eighty percent of my customers, including your aunt, have the older kind. An electric alarm clock is what it amounts to. When it goes off, salt water from the brine tank flows into the mineral tank and the treated water goes into the hot-water heater."

"What time was my aunt's set to activate?"

"You expect me to remember that? I've got two hundred and fifteen customers."

"Sorry, I just thought you might—"

"Midnight, the tenth of every month." He stretched across the table to punch her lightly on the forearm.

She leaned back, taking her arm out of range. "And today's the ninth. So someone changed the day and hour."

"Unless I'm lying." Now his hand invaded her side of the table to grab her wrist and stroke it with a thumb. He'd probably read about that move in a Harlequin romance.

Pretending she needed the wrist to lift her beer, she shook off his grip. "I don't think you're lying. I have a pretty good idea who did this."

"Ooo, already? I do like a fast woman."

Maxey made herself sip beer and gaze serenely at the action beyond the glass, where men and women of all ages rumbled balls at spastic pins.

"So who's the culprit, Ms. Columbo? And how do you know?"

"I don't know for certain. So I'd rather not say."

The face that flashed through her suspicions was male, fuzzy-cheeked, the nose peeling from too much sun, the eyes always avoiding her eyes—a composite of blood brothers Curtis and Lance. She could just hear them snuffling with laughter as they dumped the dye into the tank, elbowing each other, thinking how this would scare old Maxey so bad that she'd hop the next wagon west. And stop upsetting poor Mom/Mrs. Shank.

The waitress, a top-heavy young woman in a short brown uniform, brought their burgers. Fishing a catsup bottle out of her apron pocket, she commanded them to enjoy and then bustled off.

The only other couple in the room, androgynous teens in black leather, with spiky haircuts and nose rings, thumbed a coin into the little jukebox on their table to add heavy-metal rock to the ambience. Maxey thought about swallowing a pair of aspirin as preventative medicine.

"Francis, why didn't you tell me that you knew my mother?"

She'd caught him with a mouthful of hamburger. He wiped his chin with his napkin. His upper lip still gleamed with grease.

"I didn't tell you?"

"Come on, you know you didn't. It would have been the most natural thing, when we met, if you'd said, 'Oh, yeah, Peggy's girl.' Why didn't you?"

His eyes got big, his mouth grinned, and she knew he was going to say something dumb.

"I was too embarrassed, her and I being such passionate lovers. I was afraid you'd find out anyway—and you did—so that's why I put the dye in the softener, to distract you. But you've caught me. Redhanded." His guffaw ended in a choke that made the teens twist around to stare.

Maxey sighed. "Francis, did you so much as date my mother?"

His still-watering eyes looked directly into her frowning ones. "Pursue the mother when I could have the daughter? Not likely."

Maxey slapped the top of the table so hard, her palm went numb. "You don't have the daughter. You never, ever will. Stop playing games with me and give me a straight answer when I ask you a serious question. I'm trying to establish whether you and my mother were friends. I want to know if you can tell me anything about her that I don't already know—something that will help me find the bastard who shot her."

The teens squirmed into more comfortable positions to watch the show.

Chastened, Francis centered his half-eaten hamburger on his plate, wiped both his hands with the napkin, set that down, too, folded his hands in his lap, and leaned across the table. "I delivered water softener. She said maybe a dozen words to me, half of which were *hello* and most of the rest were *good-bye*. She was about as damned frigid-rigid as you are. Do you want another beer?"

"No thank you. And thank you for really talking to me for a change."

"You're welcome."

They both picked up their sandwiches, bit, and chewed, synchronized eaters in the hamburger event. The teens continued to watch, not wanting to miss the next exciting outburst.

"We're practicing a play," Maxey said to them, twirling her finger to indicate they should turn around. "Leave us your names and we'll get you some free passes."

Everyone ate in silence for a while. Maxey broke down first, laughing as she set aside the burger. "Francis, do you know what a pill you are?"

"I guess that's why women find me hard to swallow."

Before he could expand that line into something embarrassing, she hastened to head him off. "Give me one more straight answer, please. Did your father know my mother?"

"No. Is that straight enough for you?"

It was straight enough, but it might not be true enough. She rubbed at her head, wishing she'd taken the aspirin, trying to recall what else she wanted to ask.

"Oh, yeah," she said. "Janet's neighbor thought she saw your truck in Janet's drive the day my mother was killed."

"Is that a question?"

She nodded wearily.

"Too bad. You used up your one more straight answer when you asked about my dad knowing your mom."

"If I had requested two more straight answers, what would this one have been?"

"I wasn't anywhere near your house that day. Now do you want to see the clue I found?"

That got her attention. "Clue?"

He shifted onto one hip to extract a scrap of dirty white card-board from a back pocket. "Ta-dah." He used his fist to smooth the scrap flat on the table between them. "Guess where I found this?"

Maxey squinted at the small type. "Keene Memorial Library, Fremont. Lance Chalmers's library card. Okay, where did you find it?" But she had already guessed.

"On our driveway, about where your Ford Escort was parked. Must have lost it out of his pocket when he hauled out the screw-driver he used on the back window."

"I can't say I'm surprised, but I'm definitely disappointed. You didn't find Curtis Shank's library card, too, did you?"

Drinking beer, he shook his head.

"They're too old to be pulling such dumb stunts." She threw her napkin on her plate, appetite gone.

"I bet you think they flummoxed the water. You sure it wasn't me?"

"You weren't in the house long enough to open a kazillion little bottles of red dye." She would have to talk to them. Not something she'd enjoy putting at the top of her things-to-do list.

The leather twins slithered out of their booth and swaggered past Maxey and Francis. "Your play sucks, man," one said. "Needs more sex and violence," said the other.

Francis opened his mouth to answer, and Maxey beat him to the draw. "I have to get home, Francis. Aunt Janet isn't feeling so good after this afternoon's scare. I need to be there." She stood up and searched through her shoulder bag for her wallet.

Francis gazed at her with what he probably would have classified as a lazy smile. Catsup on his chin rather spoiled the effect. "When do you want to get together again?"

"I really don't want to waste your time. My vacation's over in a few days, and I doubt if I'll be coming back."

"I might go to Colorado. You never know."

He said it like a promise, but she felt it like a threat. For an awful moment, she pictured herself arriving at the *Regard* office and finding Francis and Clark, arms draped over the backs of their chairs, coffee cups at hand, getting along famously, discussing a three-way partnership.

"I'm buying," Francis said, totally unnerving her until she realized he meant the hamburgers.

■

Curtis and Lance were somewhere else, Maxey was glad to find when she arrived home. Always put off till tomorrow what you dread to do today—maybe you'll die in your bed tonight and never have to do it.

Scotty had disconnected the water softener. Janet had scoured the bathroom sink. The whole upstairs smelled of bleach.

The three of them sat around listlessly watching the late-night news, and then they dragged off to bed, Janet making a big production of locking all the doors. Maxey hoped Curtis had a key.

Lying in bed with moonlight silvering the room, she began her nightly ritual of worrying till she fell asleep.

First on the agenda was Curtis and Lance. Why were they so anxious for Maxey to drop her inquiries? To protect Janet, who obviously hated any reference to her sister's death? Was there more to

Janet's distaste than the simple pain of recalling the awful details? Could Janet know who killed Peggy, and know very well that it wasn't Deon?

Or maybe the boys were trying to help Richard Chalmers, who seemed as set against Maxey's sleuthing as Janet was. Peggy's lover, turned killer?

Groaning, Maxey flopped over on her stomach and played the flip side of her worries. She remembered the apocryphal scene involving Francis, Clark, and the *Regard*. Then she thought of every dumb thing that Reece had ever wanted to do to "improve" the newspaper: the contest to see which reader could find the most typographical errors; the comic strip he wanted to base on the adventures of a pet rock; the remodeling project to glass in the whole front of the office so that people on the mall could watch them work; the guard snake he wanted to get to patrol the premises at night. For all Maxey knew, he'd instituted every one of these changes in her absence.

She made up her mind to phone Reece in the morning and to confront Curtis and Lance as soon as possible, and then she relaxed enough to sleep.

■

Stretching the cord to reach from counter to kitchen table, Maxey dialed the *Regard*. Her second cup of breakfast coffee had cooled enough to sip. As far as she could tell, no one else had struggled out of bed yet, in spite of the midmorning hour. Seeing the bathroom plumbing cough up red water had left everyone feeling—no better word for it—drained.

Maxey frowned as the phone rang a sixth time. Reece answered before the seventh, his "Hello" compressed into a single syllable.

"Hey. How about a polite 'This is the *Blatant Regard*, Reece Macy speaking; how may I help you?' "

"Hey, yourself. How's Nebraska?"

"Fine. Is everything under control at the office?"

"Sure. Why? Did you hear something?"

Maxey, who had just decided to relax against the back of her chair, changed her mind and straightened up instead. "What would I have heard? Something bad happened?"

"Oh, no, no. We're doing fine. Great. The paper was only one day late."

"Reece! You guys didn't make the Wednesday-afternoon deadline?"

"Not quite, but it's cool. The paper is ready for distribution today, looking good. Maybe the delay will shake up our readers, make them appreciate us and our usual dependability more."

"Are you going to meet the deadline next week?"

"Sure, no problem."

It took all Maxey's willpower to hold back the lecture that Reece wouldn't have listened to anyway. "Anything else I should know?" she asked instead.

"Let's see. There was someone asking for you the other afternoon—a friend."

"Oh? Who?" Maxey put her anger on hold.

"Good-looking dude. I'm trying to remember his name."

"Yeah, yeah. If you think you can tease me into forgiving—"

"Calen Taylor."

Maxey did find forgiveness in her heart. "He is a good-looking dude, isn't he? Did he say what he wanted?"

"Well, uh, actually, he was here on official business. He was helping to put out the fire."

"What!"

"No damage done. Just a little wastebasket fire. Clark has promised never to dump an ashtray again without checking that all the butts are dead."

"You tell him his butt is dead if he smokes in the office anymore. You didn't tell me he smokes. He can't smoke in the office. It's bad for the computer, to say nothing of human beings. I don't want my hair and clothes to smell like a pool hall every night when I come home from a hard day of getting the news out on time."

When she finally shut up, she found Reece was talking, too, and probably hadn't heard a word after "can't smoke."

"Says he was planning to give it up anyway. I'm sure it won't be a prob—"

"Anything else you need to confess, Reece? Perhaps an obscene word on the front page that'll cause all our subscribers to cancel?"

"You want me to mail you a copy so you can see for yourself what a great issue it turned out to be?"

"Yes, that would be nice. Do you need the address?"

"It's in the Rolodex on your desk, right? I'm sure I'll be able to read it after it dries out."

"Reece!"

"Kidding. Just kidding. You relax and have fun in Nebraska."

"Big news—my father's alive." She waited in vain for his reaction to her melodramatic announcement.

The line remained open and silent.

"Reece, did you hear what I said?"

His voice came too loud in her ear. "Gotta go, Maxey."

"What's wrong?"

"Nothing. Just a little problem in the rest room. Have we got one of those suction thingies on a stick around here anywhere?"

"I don't—"

"Gotta go."

"Don't remodel anything. No snakes!"

Reece wasn't on the line anymore.

Janet shuffled into the kitchen. Without makeup, her burgundy hair in limp disarray, Janet looked all of however many years she'd lived and a few that she hadn't.

"Sit down and I'll fix you some coffee," Maxey urged.

Her aunt ignored the offer, rooting through a lower cabinet to bring forth a Bundt pan. "Gotta make Scotty's cake before the day gets hot."

"I'll help. What kind does he want?"

"Chocolate–chocolate bit, with chocolate icing."

"A man after my own heart."

"A man after empty calories."

The back stairs thumped with heavy feet, and Curtis emerged, hair tousled, eyes unfocused, smelling of sweat and unbrushed teeth. He lifted a Wheaties box off the top of the refrigerator.

Without enthusiasm, Janet considered the boxes and sacks she'd assembled on the counter. "Guess I'll get dressed first." Her steps creaked overhead as Curtis settled down at the table with his cereal.

"So, Curt," Maxey said, "what have you and Lance got planned for today?"

He wasn't awake enough to be suspicious of the question. "School. Then I gotta install a new fan belt in the Mustang."

Maxey leaned against the chilly wall of the refrigerator, trying to decide her next move. She could ask Curtis about the vandalized Ford and the ruined water softener now, before the sugar in his bowl woke him to wary awareness. She could probably surprise some honest answers out of him. But then she'd have lost that element of surprise by the time she confronted Lance, and it was Lance, after all, on whom she had the goods. Better to wait till she could beard both boys at once in whichever den they happened to be.

Scotty trotted downstairs and hit the kitchen smiling.

"Happy birthday," Maxey said. "And many, many more."

He struck a pose, hand over his heart. "I'm in the prime of senility." Then he rubbed his freshly shaved jaw. "So prime, I can't even remember who it is I'm quoting."

When Janet came down again, her face and hair looked better, though not as fresh as her pink gingham dress. She accepted the coffee Maxey handed her and drank it standing up, scanning the recipe for Scotty's cake.

"Do you mind if we don't go anywhere today, Maxey? I have some chores to do, errands to run."

"Of course not. You shouldn't feel you need to entertain me. Give me some of your chores to do."

"No, no. Well, I guess you could call Francis Coffman and tell him to come get his softener tank."

"He knows about the incident. I'm sure he'll be stopping by with a new—"

"I don't want a new one. I don't want to worry about what's in every drop—acid, lye, pesticide, LSD, whatever."

"Even cinnamon," Scotty spoke up. "I hate cinnamon."

But before Maxey could call Francis, before they'd finished their breakfast of orange juice and toast, he arrived in his van. He'd brought not only a new brine tank and salt pellets but also a sleek new mineral tank with an electronic timer in a clear lock-down cover.

"We use these at apartment houses where the kids might horse around with the equipment," he said, ignoring Janet's demands that he shovel the whole "kit-caboodle" out the back door and send her a final bill.

It took him forty minutes and much banging around before he called Janet and Scotty to come see how the new one worked. Having set the timer for midnight the tenth of every month, he locked the front and flourished the key into Janet's hand.

He winked at Maxey, who stood looking on from the kitchen. "Now all you have to worry about is fire, tornadoes, and earthquakes."

Janet turned away, looking at the key in her hand, her face sour and sagging. Maxey wondered if she, too, suspected Curtis and Lance. And if she did, was this better or worse than fearing that Peggy's killer had visited the scene of the crime again?

12

...

The day had begun partly sunny, but it had deteriorated to partly cloudy by the time Maxey drove through Gruder on her way to the cemetery. This pilgrimage was another thing to do that she'd been putting off—visiting her mother's grave. The armload of white and yellow chrysanthemums Janet had urged her to bring along from the backyard filled the car with their sharp weedy stink.

It was a short trip. Gruder had provided an acre of flat, treeless ground on a road behind the Christian Church for their dead. Maxey stopped the Escort in the side ditch. There wasn't a drive-way through the burial plots. The black iron fence seemed not as much to contain the cemetery as to hold off the corn that crowded in on three sides.

Wild golden grain tickled Maxey's legs as she picked her way to the gate. Of course the hinges creaked when she pushed through. A blackbird shouted at her from his perch on an eroded stone grave marker. She felt like a character in Poe.

She remembered the graveside service taking place at the far left side, somewhere near the back. Walking in that direction, she realized she'd forgotten the flowers in the backseat. She'd find the grave first and go back for them.

She waded through the uncut grass, thinking of spiders and chiggers. Were there snakes in Nebraska? The wind gusted from nowhere and lifted her bangs, cooling her sweaty forehead.

The mottled rose marble of her mother's marker bided beside the northern fencerow. PEGGY WITTER BURN, it read, the last three letters obscured by an empty green memorial can leaning against them. It was a single stone on a single plot, with no room for someone else to lie beside her someday. No other Witters occupied adjacent plots. Peggy in death was as aloof as she'd been in life.

"Hi, Mom," Maxey said, feeling as self-conscious as if she was not absolutely alone here.

Now what? She wasn't religious, so praying would be hypocritical. What else did one do when one visited the dead? Cry? What good would that do?

"How about you tell me who shot you?" Maxey circled around to sit on the corner edge of the tombstone.

The peekaboo sun slid under a long, ominous cloud bank. The wind played rougher.

"I'm just going to rest here awhile and think, okay? If you want to help me, jump right in. I keep an open mind about ghosts and supernormal stuff."

Elbows on knees, chin on hands, Maxey shut her eyes. First, let's rule out the people who didn't kill Peggy Burnell. Not Deon Burnell, for sure. Not Scotty Springer, who wasn't even here then. Not Curtis or Lance, because they were too young. Not Janet, because— well, she loved Peggy.

The narrow stone under her thighs was suddenly unbearable. Standing, she brushed at her bottom and went to lean on the fence instead. She shut her eyes again, the better to see.

Not Francis, probably. He's awful, but not evil, and I really don't think he knew Mom well enough to shoot her. Probably his dad didn't either, but I really ought to research that.

Richard Chalmers? Because Richard and Peggy were lovers? Inez Chalmers? Because Richard and Peggy were lovers? Because Inez and Peggy were lovers? Let's not get carried away here. Mom's best friend, Sophie Otis? Sophie's husband, Dennis? Because of the big secret Sophie thinks Peggy knew?

If Sophie's theory is right, maybe a stranger did the killing. Maybe Mom witnessed a gangland crime, and then a hit man came in, did his business, and left town.

Or maybe there was no secret. Maybe the killer was some psychopath on his way across country, picking a victim at random.

No, because that wouldn't explain the sinister black truck that tried to crowd Janet off the road. And Curtis and Lance wouldn't have gone that far in their dirty tricks, even if I myself had been driving that day.

A mosquito whined past her ear, and Maxey flailed it off, trying not to lose her train of thought.

Talk to Lance and Curtis. And Tommy Coffman. Also, Inez and Richard Chalmers. Talk to Dr. Otis—alone. Ask one and all if they know a secret. Five days I've got left here. I can solve this. I'm lots better at deadlines than Reece is.

She batted her eyes open and pulled up straight. "I brought you some flowers, Mom. Be right back."

Watching the ground so as not to fall over anyone's headstone or step on anyone's potted plant, Maxey wound back through the cemetery. She didn't lift her head till she got to the gate, and there was Lance, sitting on the hood of her car. The Chalmerses' black truck nosed close behind the Ford.

After one misstep of surprise, Maxey strode on out to greet him. "Hey. What're you doing in this neck of the plains?"

He nodded without answering, chewing something that swelled

his cheek. She hoped it was gum and not tobacco. He looked perfect with her ramshackle car—thready cutoff jeans, a T-shirt without sleeves, black gym shoes without laces, his jaw dirty with a few days' whiskers.

He looked down at his hands, loose between his knees. "Can we talk for a minute?"

"Sure."

"I don't want to, see, but I have to. Talk to you, I mean."

She nodded, folding her arms. "I know exactly what you mean."

"See, things have gotten a little out of hand since you came to Gruder. I can understand your wanting to know who . . . did that to your mother. But what good would it do her or you? And you don't realize the . . . the bad that you might do—to Janet, and Curtis. And everybody."

"Explain it to me."

He rolled his shoulders, wiped one hand down his face, stared up the road. "I can't. It's a secret."

In spite of the heat, Maxey's arms prickled with goose bumps. "Whose secret is it?"

"I can't tell you that. I shouldn't even be talking to you."

"Lance, you may be talking to me, but you aren't saying anything. Do you know who killed my mother? Is that it?"

"No! But whoever it was, you shouldn't be stirring them up."

"Okay. Let's accept, for the moment, that you don't know who killed her. Do you know why she was killed?"

"How could I know that? Do you?" Lance had apparently gone to the same school of useless circulatory conversation as Francis Coffman.

Sighing with exasperation, Maxey dug into her shorts pocket. "I suppose you also don't know who vandalized my car while it was parked at the Coffman place." She hoped she had the library card with her.

"This was a bad idea," Lance said, sliding off the hood and turning toward his truck.

"Hold it." Maxey waved the battered card in triumph. "Do you recognize exhibit A?"

He leaned halfheartedly to see and drew back as if it had bitten him.

"This was found at the scene of the crime. I'm also ninety percent sure that when the police finish fingerprinting the glass bottles from the softener, they'll be able to identify you and/or Curtis as having dumped the dye in there."

She hoped her expression came across as self-righteous rather than devious. Since the police had not been notified, and the defiled water softener had disappeared in Francis's van, it seemed doubtful any fingerprint matching would take place.

Head down, Lance jammed his fists into his pockets and kicked at the graveled shoulder. "I was trying to scare you off."

"So I guessed. You and Curtis—"

"Not Curtis, just me!" He tapped his chest. "Me."

"Oh, come on, Lance. You expect me to believe that your best pal didn't know what you were doing to his pesty cousin?"

Tilting his head back, Lance spat whatever he'd been chewing in a line drive down the ditch. He twisted toward Maxey, eyes glittering. "Damn right he didn't know. I didn't need his help."

"Were you in the truck that tried to—"

"I can think for myself," he blurted, tuning her out. "I'm not a kid anymore. I'm not a goddamned kid!"

His voice cracked on the last word, spoiling the effect of his declaration.

"Lance, I don't want to file a complaint and cause you trouble, but after all, you've caused me some. The Hertz people may tear up my driver's license when they see this Ford come crawling home."

"The insurance—"

"That's not the point. The point is, you had no right to brutalize it in the first place. Or the Cloud-Sof people's property, either."

"Give me a little time," he snapped, as if she were imposing upon him. "I'll work out some restitution."

"You think your dad will help?"

"No. Just don't say anything to anyone, okay?"

Maxey could imagine Inez rescuing her son with a few thousand dollars, the two of them keeping the problem from Richard Chalmers. Keeping it a *secret.*

In all the time they'd stood talking, no traffic had passed on the road. Now two pickups—one red and one blue—rattled by in rapid succession. Maxey took the opportunity to study Lance as he watched them pass, his hand raised in recognition. Under the dirt and whiskers, he looked too pale and very young.

"See you," he mumbled, turning again toward his truck.

"How'd you know I was here?" Maxey asked, walking around her own vehicle, intending to retrieve the flowers.

"Saw you coming out of the Shank's lane as I was coming up the road to help Curt with the Mustang. Followed you on the chance we could have a conversation."

"Yes, well I'm glad we had this little talk. Emphasis on *little,"* Maxey said, reaching for the door handle.

"Oh." Lance stopped in his tracks, holding up one hand. "I have to tell you. At first, when I saw you were way off in the cemetery, it seemed too good an opportunity, you know?"

Maxey shook her head. "Opportunity?"

"To scare you again," he said. His mouth twitched into an abashed smile before he strode to the truck and hurled himself inside.

"Lance!" she yelled impotently as he swerved out around her and accelerated down the road.

She circled the Ford, checking that all the tires were intact. Then with some trepidation, she opened the driver's side door and peered inside.

The smell of chrysanthemums boiled out to greet her. In her absence, there had been a flower explosion. Diminutive particles of yellow and white and green covered the backseat, the front seat, the floors. Some even clung to the fuzzy felt ceiling.

After staring at the mess for half a minute, Maxey brushed a clean space on the driver's seat, slid in, and drove sedately away. She spent much of the short trip home replaying what Lance had said, trying to discover the hidden meanings. The only new idea that occurred to her was that Lance, in the midst of his burning emotion, had not looked angry so much as he'd looked scared down to his rubber-clad toes.

■

"Happ-ee birth-day to yoooou." Three untrained voices trailed away and then laughed in better unison than they had sung. Scotty applauded before bending forward to blow out the dozen candles—all, Janet claimed, that she could afford.

Maxey studied the white-and-blue sugared number embedded in the icing. "Seventy-one? What is that, your bowling average?"

"Anyone who doesn't like chocolate can leave the table," Janet said, handing Scotty a wedge-shaped knife.

"Anyone who doesn't like chocolate needs therapy," Curtis said. He chewed at the fingernail of one little finger while he watched Scotty carve the cake.

"Come on, Scotty—you aren't seventy-one," Maxey insisted.

"You think I'm so old I don't know my own age?" He mock-glared at her. "When my friends begin to flatter me about how young I look, that's when I know I'm getting old. Mark Twain said something like that."

Janet stretched to smack Scotty lightly on his chest. "Maxey didn't say you looked young; she said you couldn't be seventy-one. There're other interpretations of that observation."

Scotty offered Janet a plate piled with cake, one green candle sinking in the quicksand of gooey dark icing. "Sweets for the caustic," he said.

For Maxey, this was the perfect end to an imperfect day. After an afternoon communing with the dead, it felt invigorating to celebrate a birth.

When the cake lay in ruins, Janet went into the pantry and came back bearing presents. "If you can guess what it is, you can have it," she said, setting the three colorfully shrouded offerings beside his plate.

"Gosh, what could this be?" Scotty held up what was obviously the size, shape, and weight of a hardcover book.

"Yes, but you have to tell what the title is," Maxey said, laughing.

"It's that Madonna photo book," Curtis guessed.

Janet set a full glass of milk in front of him and settled in her chair again. "Don't be silly. Scotty isn't religious-minded, and Maxey isn't, either."

Maxey and Curt exchanged surreptitious amused looks.

"*History Through Maps.*" Scotty held it aloft. "This looks real interesting."

"So does Madonna," Curtis murmured.

He wasn't usually so talkative, and Maxey had never heard him joke about anything. He obviously hadn't heard from Lance since Maxey accused them of malicious mischief. She hated to spoil his good mood, but she really should take advantage of his blissful ignorance. Get him alone and ask for his version of Lance's story.

"What in hell is this? A cellular phone? Good gosh, Jannie. Do I need this?"

"I can call you to bring home a loaf of bread. If you're in an accident, you can get help. And, oh, there're lots of uses."

"Well, thank you, I think."

Janet wadded up the wrapping paper. "It'll grow on you."

"Yeah," Curtis said. " 'Cause isn't that the kind of phone that's supposed to give people brain cancer?"

"Oh, hush," Janet grumbled. "I'll bet you wouldn't turn it down if someone offered one to you."

"Hey, Curt, my man," Scotty said, holding up the T-shirt he'd just unwrapped.

Neon purple, with chartreuse letters, it proclaimed *Don't engage me in a battle of wits; I'm unarmed.* Maxey and Janet hooted and laughed.

Curtis hunched over his plate of cake, obviously pleased and embarrassed. "You can use it to polish the Bronco or something."

The telephone rang. Before anyone else could react, Maxey jumped up, unreasonably certain that it was Lance about to warn his friend that she was onto them. "I'll get it. I'm closest."

A breathy little voice asked for Curtis. Wondering if Lance's ability for troublemaking included a talent for female impressions, Maxey pointed the receiver at Curtis.

He scrambled up and, having exchanged hellos with the caller, stretched the cord around the dining room doorway to converse out of sight and in private. Maxey, putting one and one together, figured this young lady explained Curtis's good mood at dinner.

"Tomorrow's Saturday. What shall we do with it?" Janet asked. "How about if we go over to the DeSoto Wildlife Refuge?"

"I'm easy. Sounds good," Maxey said.

Scotty reached to the far end of the table to pull out a triple A book. He flipped pages, right to the one he wanted. " 'Contains seven thousand eight hundred and twenty-three acres of the Missouri River floodplain divided between Iowa and Nebraska. . . . Seven-hundred-and-fifty-acre DeSoto Lake . . . the woodlands shelter deer, raccoons, coyotes, and nesting songbirds.' None of which will show their noses while we're cruising the grounds."

"It's not very far. Just across the Iowa line on Highway Thirty," Janet said.

Maxey, still trying—unsuccessfully—to eavesdrop on Curtis, nodded and smiled.

Scotty snapped the book shut and fished a toothpick out of his shirt pocket. "The neatest thing they got is this wreck of a steamboat that they found buried in a farmer's field."

This got Maxey's full attention. "How'd it get there?"

"Apparently in the late 1800s, when the steamboat sank, the Missouri River went a different way than it does now. It cut itself a new channel, left the old one—and the lost boat—high and dry."

"Neat. I want to see that."

Curtis strolled into the kitchen again, smirking at the floor. He hung up the telephone, then stood scratching one bent elbow.

Maxey jumped up again. "Since it's Scotty's birthday, and Janet did the magnificent-as-always cooking, Curt and I will wash dishes."

"Hey." Curtis came to attention. "I got a date tonight."

"What time?" Maxey gathered plates.

"Eight."

"Nearly two hours off. We'll be done in twenty minutes, easy."

Out the corner of her eye, Maxey saw him wanting to whine, but Janet sent him a keen look full of motherly warning, and he grabbed up a handful of dirty silverware instead.

Standing, Scotty yanked his new purple T-shirt on over his old navy one. Picking up the cellular phone and the map book, he led Janet toward the living room and the TV.

"Okay." Curtis sighed, taking a dish towel out of a drawer and waiting resolutely. "What did you want to talk about?"

"You're very perceptive."

"No, you're very nosy."

Maxey turned on the hot water and relaxed as it ran out clear. "And you're very thoughtless. Scaring your poor mother with that red dye stunt."

"I didn't do that."

"I'll bet you know who did, then."

"Nope. Not a clue." He flipped the tea towel one way and then another, fidgeting like a bridegroom.

"I was talking to Lance today."

"God! Leave the guy alone, can't you?"

She shifted around to stare him in the eye. "As it happens, he came looking for me. Followed me to the cemetery. To talk."

"Yeah? What about?"

"Well, we discussed my poor rental car, for one thing."

Maxey flinched as Curtis swatted the counter with the towel. "That dumb . . . dummy. What'd he want to talk about that for?"

"His conscience was bothering him, I guess. Francis found Lance's library card in the Coffman's driveway." Maxey scrubbed the daylights out of a blue glass bowl for a minute or so, waiting for Curtis's next comment.

In the living room, Janet whooped an uninhibited laugh at something Scotty or the television said, oblivious to her son's distress.

"You going to press charges?" Curtis mumbled.

"Not if you tell me the truth. You were there, weren't you?"

"Yeah. The two of us. It was great. Didn't you ever want to trash a car?"

She handed him the blue bowl, and he automatically began to dry it. "And your reason?" she asked.

"We wanted you to back off. Drop this obsession with who knocked off your mother. Hoped you'd piss your pants and go home. Isn't that the same thing Lance said?"

"Essentially," Maxey said, stung that Curtis could be deliberately rude and cruel to his oh-so-reasonable cousin. "And you wanted me to back off because you know who killed her and you want to protect him or her?"

"No! Did Lance say that?"

"Not in so many words. He hinted there is this secret—"

Curtis groaned. "There's no secret. Okay? We don't know who killed your mother. Okay? The only reason I got Lance to help me destroy your car was because you're driving Mom crazy digging into the past. You aren't going to find out shit because the experts—the sheriff and those guys—didn't find out shit. So why stir up all this shit that's hurting my mother?"

She rounded on him, giving in to her own anger. "Because she accused my dad of murdering my mother. Do you know how that makes me feel?"

"Yes," he almost yelled. "Yes," he said scarcely above a whisper. "I do. My dad—" Curtis drew a shaky breath and huffed it out. "He beat my mother to death."

Maxey shook her head, trying to clear her mind.

"My real father," he explained with uncharacteristic patience. "He abused my real mother. I was born early after his last attack. Her last attack. She died the next day."

Maxey continued to shake her head, eyes burning, wanting to put her arms around him but knowing he'd rebuff her.

"So, see, Maxey, I understand."

"The difference is, my father didn't do it. I can't bear for people, especially the people who loved Mom, to think he's responsible."

Curtis gazed across the room with unseeing eyes. "If my mother had lived, he'd have gone on hurting her. He'd have abused me, too. I hate it that she died, but there's worse things could have happened. Worse things could come from your insisting on finding your mother's killer, too."

Maxey turned back to the sink, lifting a stack of cups into the cooling dishwater. "Your mother and dad. Are you sure he mistreated her? Isn't that just hearsay? From people you thought you could trust? What would you do if you found out he wasn't anywhere near her the day you were born?"

Curtis shifted impatiently beside her. Through the window screen in front of them, a breeze redolent of manure blotted the sweat from Maxey's forehead.

"You feel bad now," she added. "How would you feel then?"

"Leave us alone." Curtis hurled the towel against the refrigerator. "Why can't you leave us the hell alone?" He stamped across the kitchen floor, ripped open the screen door, and let it bang shut behind him.

In a few moments, the Mustang roared to life and scattered gravel on its way to the road.

Maxey continued to wash dishes, pausing every now and then to swipe at her nose with the back of her wrist, determined not to give up and cry.

By the time she'd dried the last pan, it was pitch-black outside, and she felt like a sitting duck, framed in the lighted window.

13

. . .

Except for an encounter with Richard Chalmers, Maxey's weekend was a pleasure.

First thing Saturday morning, she hunted up her notebook with its puny list of questions about her mother's death. Feeling the pressure of time's passage, she considered calling Dr. Otis, then decided it would be better to catch him at the office Monday than at home, where Sophie might hear and be hurt by Maxey's line of questioning. Unable to think of any promising new leads to add to the list, she snapped the book shut and went downstairs to another too-hearty breakfast.

For the day's entertainment, Janet and Scotty took Maxey to the DeSoto National Wildlife Refuge. The first wave of migrating ducks and geese battered the sky above DeSoto Lake. Scotty spotted an eagle in the top of a cottonwood tree, and Maxey and Janet glimpsed it before it swooped away to somewhere else. As promised, the wreck of the *Bertrand* stern-wheeler was on display, its discovery and excavation summarized on signboards.

Afterward, they drove north an hour to Sioux City for midafternoon lunch at a Holiday Inn. They tried to find the city museum, but Scotty made a wrong turn, and by the time they knew where they were, they'd lost interest in looking at any more historical artifacts. Halfway home, they drove under a little rain cloud that spotted the windshield and scudded on.

The three of them played gin rummy at the kitchen table till one o'clock Sunday morning.

Janet and Scotty managed to get up early enough to go to church. Maxey didn't.

In the afternoon, the three of them walked to downtown Gruder for the annual Colonial Days—a flea market, carnival, ice cream social, and street dance rolled into one hot, noisy festivity. Scotty and Janet spent most of their time square-dancing to recorded music and a live hand-clapping caller. The latter reminded Maxey of ZZ Top. His bushy gray beard needed pruning.

Maxey wandered the aisles of booths—games of chance interspersed by tables of arts and crafts for sale. She noticed a ceramic cat doorstop that might have been modeled after Moe, and she bent to study it closer.

"Hello, Colorado," a male voice boomed behind her.

She straightened and looked around at Richard Chalmers, who beamed at her and dropped his hand on her shoulder.

"Hello, Nebraska," Maxey answered, craning to see around him. "Where's Inez?"

"She's home. Didn't feel good today."

"Oh, that's too bad. Is she—"

"Had any ice cream yet?" Richard asked, kneading Maxey's upper arm.

"No. Is it good?" She hated the sly intimacy of his grip, but she didn't want to antagonize him by pulling away. She needed to talk to him first. Feeling hypocritical in the third degree, she smiled at him. "Is it homemade?"

"Come on. I'll buy you a cone." His arm tightened around her shoulder and wheeled her into an about-face.

They strolled the middle of the street, Richard raising his free hand every now and then to greet a friend. Maxey thought the ratio ran about two to one in favor of females.

"Ask you a question?" She waved, herself, at the elderly twins from the sewing circle.

"If it's anything to do with investments and annuities, I charge fifty bucks an hour."

She pretended to laugh. His patronizing arm was getting heavy. "I just wondered if you have any theories about my mother's murder."

She felt him stiffen, but he didn't miss a step. "Come on, honey. You don't want to spoil a beautiful day with that kind of conversation. Do you think the Colorado Buffs can beat the Nebraska Cornhuskers next season?"

"I've got this idea that you know something about the murder that you didn't tell the sheriff. Why else would you be so set against my inquiries? You and Janet and Lance and Curtis and maybe Inez all seem awfully nervous about—"

"You leave us out of this." He yanked his arm away from her and came to a full stop. "Leave me and my family alone. We might have our suspicions, but we don't know diddly-squat about the whole sorry business."

"What will it hurt to tell me your suspicions, then? I won't share them with anyone else. I can keep a *secret.*"

He didn't react to the last word, which she'd emphasized. He was still back at the word *hurt.*

"What hurts is to scrape up the past," he said. "You've got to forget your mother and move on with your life." He shoved his hands into his pants pockets and began striding along the street, ignoring everyone on either side.

Maxey had to jog to keep up. "Where were you the afternoon she died?"

He stopped so suddenly, she trotted four paces beyond and had to walk back for his answer.

"I don't recall. I do know—I'm absolutely certain—I was not in your aunt's living room firing a bullet into your mother's brain." He began to walk back the way they'd come, shouting over his shoulder, "You can get your own ice cream. I've lost my appetite."

Several curious faces swiveled to look at Maxey. She hastened off in the opposite direction, angry with Chalmers for being such a jerk and with herself for failing to learn anything new.

Heading home, she glimpsed Curtis and Lance joking and jostling through the crowd, a small pack of slender young women laughing at their heels. For a few self-indulgent seconds, Maxey was angry at all of them, too.

Sunday night, Janet and Scotty and Maxey played poker till well after midnight. Scotty trounced the ladies, but since they were betting pennies, his winnings didn't put him in another income-tax bracket.

■

"So what do you want to do today?" Janet asked Monday morning, carrying her coffee cup to the kitchen table and sitting down opposite Maxey.

Maxey shook her head. "How about nothing? You've been entertaining me too well. I don't know how much more I can take."

Janet sat up straighter and test-touched her cranberry hair, obviously pleased at the idea she could outlast her younger niece. "We have to get everything in. No telling when you'll ever be back for another visit. It took you so long to schedule this one."

Scotty came in through the screen door, a galvanized bucket swinging in one hand. He whistled his way to the sink, squirted two blobs of dish detergent into the bucket, and headed outside again.

"Maxey, want me to wash your Ford while I'm doing the Bronco?" he called back through the screen.

She laughed. "That would be like putting a Band-Aid on a broken leg. No thanks. I think when I deliver that poor car to the rental agency, clean or not, they'll probably just shoot it."

Janet sipped at her coffee, her eyes blank with preoccupation. "We could spend the day at a casino."

"How about I help you clean house or do a laundry or whatever needs doing around here?" Maxey suggested. "Pay you back a little."

Janet pushed a forefinger into the air. "Heartland of America Park, in downtown Omaha. Fountains, boat rides, a light show."

Maxey sighed. "If that's what you really want to do."

An outside faucet squeaked open and water hit the bucket.

"If we're lucky, they may have a concert scheduled," Janet said. "How about if we go after lunch?"

"Sure. Janet, if you don't care, I'm going to call the *Regard* office on my credit card again."

"Oh, pooh. You worry too much."

"I hope so."

■

Maxey made the call while Janet was outside using a canister vacuum cleaner on the Bronco's interior. The telephone rang on and on. She glanced at her watch. Ten after eleven, Colorado time. Okay, was Reece taking an early lunch or had he overslept this late?

"Hello *Regard* help you?" His fast breaths snuffled into her ear.

"Sounds as if I caught you at a bad time. You okay?"

"Oh, hi, Maxey. Yeah. Just using the john."

"How's this issue shaping up? You going to have it ready for Thursday?"

"Sho'nuff. Yup."

"No more fires?"

"Nope. Nope."

"And Clark? Is he working out okay?"

"Clark is gone."

"Gone?" Unsure if Reece meant out to lunch or deceased, Maxey's tongue stumbled over the next question. "How—when will he be back?"

"I fired him. Told him to keep his fortune and get out of my newspaper office."

She had to sit down in a handy kitchen chair. She couldn't believe it. "I don't believe it. What happened? Did you have a fight over his smoking?"

"No, worse. He was bringing women in here."

"What kind of women?"

"Feminine female women—with painted toenails and low-cut shoes. I came down to the office one night late to get something and found him tying one of them to my swivel chair. With, if you can picture this, my typewriter ribbon. She had on a big smile and gladiator sandals—period."

Maxey had to cover the mouthpiece fast to keep Reece from hearing her burp of laughter. Womanizer Reece? Shocked by another man's womanizing?

"So write up your proposal, Maxey. If you can pay me at least a hundred a month, maybe I'll take you up on a buyout."

"I'm sorry your plans fell through."

"Yeah, yeah."

"No, I really am. I know you want to get away from the *Regard.*"

"I'm just glad I found out about ol' Dumpster before I left you alone with him."

"Gosh, did it ever occur to you I might enjoy an orgy among the filing cabinets?"

"Anytime you want to try it, you see me first."

"Oh." She sat up straighter, hand to her forehead. "Oh no."

"What now?"

"You'll never be able to put out the newspaper alone. I'll head back right away."

"No need. I've got it covered."

"Reece, I know you want to have it under control, but optimism alone isn't going to—"

"No, I really do have it taken care of. Wait till you hear what a brilliant idea I had."

"Uh-oh." She felt she should sit down, but she was already sitting down.

"Eight high school kids are earning extra credit in journalism class by putting out this week's *Regard*. They're writing stories, getting ads, pasting up, the whole shebang. I'm sitting here all day, feet on my desk, reading *Omni*, eating a bag of potato chips, and drinking lemonade with lots of ice—except when I have to go to the john."

Maxey felt her grin stretch ear to ear. "That *is* brilliant, you big lug, you. I'm truly impressed."

"Yeah, me, too. So you stay where you are and have a good time and I'll see you later in the week."

She felt a niggle of homesickness. *Omni*, potato chips, and lemonade sounded mighty good. "Hey, Reece, maybe you've stumbled onto a genius idea here. How many journalism classes do you figure there are in the Boulder area?"

His laugh made her smile again.

The huge success of that phone call gave Maxey the confidence to try another one. She looked up the number and dialed Dr. Otis's office. A pleasant female voice answered.

"I'd like an appointment," Maxey began, suddenly realizing that she might end up paying to talk to him and doubting it would be worth the fee.

"The doctor is out of the office for two weeks on vacation. Dr. Pollock is covering for him. Would you like to see Dr. Pollock?"

"No thanks. Never mind." Maxey hung up, feeling both disappointed and relieved. She could phone or visit him if he'd stayed at home, but she really doubted either of the Otises had anything to do with Peggy's murder. That didn't fit in with the defensive efforts of Lance and Curtis. She hated to think what did fit in with their efforts.

■

"I've got a queen-size headache," Janet said. "You two go without me."

"We can't do that," Maxey said. "We'll stay home and help you."

"No. I want to be alone to suffer in peace. Go on now. I've seen the fountains."

"Come on, Maxey," Scotty said. "She'll be fine once she's had as-pirin and a nap. You and I will just have to enjoy ourselves without her."

"Well . . ." Maxey wished she'd thought of the headache first. She could have hid out in her room with a book.

She and Scotty walked out into the yard. For the first time since she'd arrived, the air smelled like fall, like a breeze out of the north and vegetation rotting.

"You just washed the Bronco. Let's take the Escort," Maxey said.

"Okay, but can I drive? Riding shotgun makes me fidgety as measles on top of chicken pox."

"Ick. By all means, drive."

Scotty circled the car, opened his door, and stared in at the chrysanthemum compost browning in the backseat.

"Don't ask," Maxey said, settling herself in the passenger side.

Shaking his head, Scotty got in and started the car. As they pulled out of the barnyard, Maxey waved at the kitchen windows in case Janet was watching.

Scotty drove a block into Gruder, pulled over into the grassy side ditch, and turned to Maxey. "Now. Where would you really like to go?"

She grinned at him. She thought about it. "Let's go up to West Point and ask Tommy Coffman if he knew my mother."

■

They were in luck. Tommy was at home and Francis wasn't.

Tommy opened the front door to them, scowling as if they'd interrupted something. But when he recognized Maxey, his face relaxed, though he didn't go so far as to smile.

"Have you got a minute to spare?" Maxey asked brightly.

"You aren't selling encyclopedias, are you?"

She shook her head. "Tommy Coffman, Scotty Springer. And vice versa."

The men shook hands with no more enthusiasm than wedding guests from opposite sides of the aisle. Tommy stepped aside and let them into the vestibule. It smelled of stale cigars.

"In here," Tommy said, leading them down two steps to a long room full of chairs, throw rugs, newspapers, and stereo equipment. The far wall was all fieldstone, with a fireplace large enough to roast a small ox.

Maxey perched on the edge of a sleek black leather sofa and the men chose equally ostentatious seating across from her. She didn't see any point in attempting small talk. Tommy would prefer she get straight to the point.

"I have a question about my mother. Did you know her?"

"No." Tommy crossed one leg over the other.

She'd been so prepared to hear yes and then to ask him more questions that the flat no, threw her into complete confusion. Eyes wide, she sent a silent, panicky appeal to Scotty.

"You probably heard about Peggy Burnell, though, when she was killed," Scotty said. "Did you hear theories about why it happened?"

Tommy rubbed the flat of a hammy hand down the side of his face. "None I recall."

"Well," Maxey said, planting her feet, ready to stand, disgusted that she hadn't asked the right question, the one that would have sent Tommy to his knees, blurting out his role in the whole sordid affair.

Scotty bounced out of his chair and crossed the room to the fireplace mantel. Hands clasped behind him, he studied a photograph in an ornate silver frame. From where Maxey sat, it looked like a group picture of guys in uniform.

"U. S. Army Air Corps." Scotty looked back at Tommy. "You piloted in World War Two?"

"Fortresses."

"Pacific?"

Tommy nodded.

"I was a ball-turret gunner," Scotty said.

"Yeah? You've got the build for it. God, I don't know how you guys could stand being wedged in that little window. I flew one of the first B-seventeen-E's at Java. The Zeros hadn't glommed on to the fact that this issue had tail armament. They kept coming around for stern attacks, and our ball-turret gunners had a field day."

Scotty laughed.

"Have a drink with me." Tommy walked purposefully toward a black leather bar that wrapped one corner of the room. "Scotch okay?"

"More than okay. ' 'Tis a consummation devoutly to be wished.' "

"How about you, Maxey?"

"Too early in the day for me, thanks."

She hated sounding like a prude, but Tommy and Scotty weren't listening to her, anyway. They convened at the bar and continued to discuss the bad old days as cheerfully as if those were the best of times. The bottle clinked against their glasses more than once.

Sighing, Maxey picked up a *Flying* magazine from the table beside her and flipped through, looking at the pictures. She'd rather be watching a fountain in Omaha.

After a bout of particularly raucous laughter, Scotty smacked the top of the bar. "Gotta be going, Tommy. Could I use your bathroom first?"

"Sure thing. Up these stairs, down the hall, second door on the left."

Maxey tossed aside the magazine and wriggled to the edge of the couch, anticipating Scotty's return. Tommy stood in the middle of the room, legs spread, arms behind his back, at parade rest.

"Is he relation of yours?" he asked, jerking his chin in the direction Scotty had gone.

"Just a friend."

"Janet Shank's fiancé or something?"

Maxey smiled. "Or something."

"Nice fella."

"Uh-huh."

"I was at the house the day your mother died."

The sudden change of subject felt like ice cubes down Maxey's back. Her smile faltered and slipped away.

"You were?"

"Sometimes I help Francis with his route, if he's on vacation or whatever. That day I had five places to service, one of them your aunt's."

Maxey tried to think what to ask him. Meanwhile, he glanced at the doorway and moved closer to her, deliberately lowering his voice.

"It was in the morning. I knocked at the back screen door and yelled who I was. The TV was blasting, and nobody answered, but the door wasn't hooked, and so I let myself in and went straight to the softener equipment there in the utility room. Only took me a minute to load in the salt pellets."

Maxey nodded.

"So I was folding up the bag, on my way out the back door, and your aunt—Janet—she came sailing into the kitchen. Saw me and stopped short. I could see I'd startled her, so I tried to apologize for it." Tommy shook his head. "She lit into me like I was Jack the Raper. Screeched and carried on. This other woman—your mother, I guess—came to see what was going on. 'This man attacked me.' That's what Janet said. I couldn't believe it. She really did think I was there to rape her. She kept ranting about it till she convinced herself I'd been close enough—crazy enough—to touch her."

Tommy massaged his temples with one spread hand across his eyes. Behind him, Scotty arrived at the top of the steps. Maxey shook her head at him, and he paused, hand on the railing.

"I didn't wait around for the police she swore she was calling," Tommy said. "If she did, they never came to get my side of it. All the way across the porch, through the yard, getting in the truck, I could hear her taking out her grievance on that other woman." He backed up to a chair and sat down.

"What do you mean? How did she take out her grievance?" Maxey prompted.

"I couldn't hear what your mother was saying, but Janet came through loud and clear. 'Don't tell me to calm down,' and 'Are you calling me a liar?' and once—" Tommy glanced at the doorway, saw Scotty, and settled back, wiping his hand across his mouth.

"It's okay," Maxey murmured. "Please go on."

"Once, I could have sworn I heard someone getting slapped."

■

"Jannie wouldn't have slapped Peggy," Scotty said. "The rest of it is probably true."

He slumped in the passenger seat of the Escort, an elbow on the armrest and chin on his hand, too full of Tommy's scotch to be fidgety about Maxey driving. She aimed the car down a gravel side road she'd chosen at random, killing time till they'd been gone long enough to have driven to Omaha and back.

"Janet seems to have some kind of rape fixation," Maxey observed tartly. "Every man she sees—"

"As best I can tell, she really was raped once."

"Oh?" The word came out harsh and doubting. Right now, Maxey's anger stood in the way of her compassion.

"As a kid. By someone who worked for her dad."

"Damn it, Scotty, life can be such a bitch." She had no doubts about that, at least.

Scotty coughed, and the smell of liquor blossomed and faded.

"So what do you think?" she asked. "How does what Tommy told me fit into my mother's last day?"

"I'd guess nowhere. Peggy probably criticized Janet for overreacting to Tommy being in the house. That made Janet all the madder. The two exchanged words. That must have been the end of it. It probably made Janet feel bad as hell later, when Peggy was dead and it was too late to make up with her. But I don't see their set-to having anything to do with Peggy being murdered."

Maxey clutched the steering wheel as the car juddered down a stretch of washboard gravel. She felt Scotty looking at her, and she stubbornly stared straight ahead.

"Janet's got some faults, but murdering folks isn't one of them," Scotty said.

■

Maxey shouldn't have drunk that last glass of iced tea before bed. It woke her two hours after she'd shut off the light and one hour after she'd finally gotten to sleep, demanding she get up and walk down the hall to the bathroom.

Groggily, she pushed her feet into her slippers, stabbed her arms into the sleeves of her robe, and tied it extra tight, since she'd skipped wearing a nightshirt that night. She shuffled into the hall. This end was black as a coal bin. The far end glowed with light from downstairs.

Turning in at the bathroom, Maxey wondered why she couldn't hear the TV. Janet or Scotty had probably fallen asleep during the late show.

She used the toilet and washed her hands without switching on the light, not wanting the glare to bring her all the way awake. She did wonder what color was coming out of the tap.

Opening the door, she listened again before turning toward her room. Something in the living room bumped softly.

Without analyzing why, she started walking in that direction. Her feet whispered down the stairs. The double doors stood far enough ajar for one person to slip through sideways. She steadied herself with a hand on one door, and it slid open wider.

Two young male faces tipped up to stare at her. Curtis and Lance sat cross-legged on the floor in the middle of the room, shoulder-to-shoulder, a spill of magazines on their knees and the rug. Maxey glimpsed an expanse of unquestionably female anatomy in the two-page spread of the magazine that Lance reflexively crushed to his chest. Curtis began gathering up the rest of the reading material, dropping most of it in his haste and having to start over.

"You don't need to patrol your area on my account," Maxey said, scratching the back of her head. "I know what naked ladies look like. Got any *Playboys* by any chance?"

The overhead light, a round sepia globe containing the silhouette of one motionless moth, didn't flatter anyone. Both Curtis and Lance looked jaundiced, their eyes underlined with dark hollows.

"It's cool," Maxey said. "I caught you with your hands in the cookie jar, but . . ." The double entendre hit her then and she couldn't help laughing.

Lance pushed himself up as if the floor had caught fire. "I've gotta go."

Curtis scrambled up even faster. "I've gotta go with you."

Lance tore his gaze away from Maxey. "No, you don't," he hooted, smacking Curtis with the girlie magazine. "You live here, numbnut." He rushed toward the dining room.

"Wait," Curtis called.

"You keep 'em."

Curtis juggled the magazines into better order, looking none too pleased with the gift.

"Sorry to break up the party," Maxey said.

Out in the barnyard, a motor ground on. It hummed the length of the driveway, roared east down the road, and the night hung silent again.

Yawning, Maxey moved toward the stairs. "Night."

When she glanced back at him, Curtis was staring at her. "What's the matter?"

He mumbled something about the view, scooped up his magazines, and fled in the opposite direction.

Maxey clutched together the lapels of her robe, embarrassed that she must have flashed the poor guys.

Under the circumstances, she couldn't help being insulted by their reaction.

■

She was wakened again, this time by the distant ringing of the telephone. Expecting someone else to get it, she plowed her head deeper into the pillow and tried to regain the dream that had been so rudely interrupted—something involving Maxey, a southern mansion, and a blond man wearing a football uniform.

The phone insisted. Throwing back the sheet, Maxey sat up and listened for a door opening or feet padding down the hall. Nothing.

Grunting, she sat up, tied on the robe, felt for her slippers, and wove her way into the hall. All the while, she expected the phone to stop. Even when she hit the kitchen light switch and grabbed at the receiver, she doubted that the caller would persist a second longer.

"Hello," she grumbled, squinting at the clock above the stove—almost two in the morning.

"Who is this?" a female voice shouted in her ear.

Drawing it away to a safer distance, Maxey frowned. She hated to talk to people on the phone who didn't know how to talk to people on the phone.

"Who did you want?" she asked as if she really cared.

"Maxey? Let me talk to Janet. Right now."

"Inez?" Alarm swept everything else from her mind. "What's the matter?"

"I want Janet. He's dead," Inez wailed. "My boy is dead."

Maxey set the receiver on the counter as if both were made of glass. She raced upstairs to get Janet, Inez's gulping sobs throbbing in her head.

14

"Why couldn't it have been one of those worthless kids who goes around selling drugs and shooting up the city?" Janet dabbed a soggy tissue at her glittering eyes. "The good do die young."

Maxey set a cup of strong hot coffee in front of her aunt, who sat in her usual chair at the kitchen table, looking alarmingly old without makeup or the red wig. Maxey didn't want to look at her real hair—short, straight, and gray-brown. It was like seeing her aunt naked.

Scotty sat beside Janet, his hand on her back. He'd donned a ragged blue seersucker robe that barely reached his knees. From the way he kept hauling at the hem, Maxey guessed he wasn't wearing anything else. She knew the feeling.

Bringing coffee for Scotty, Maxey settled at the table, chin on hand.

"It's just a miracle Curtis wasn't with him." Janet choked on the words, and she bit her lip before adding, "They were together so much."

They were probably together right now. When Maxey knocked

and called Janet out of bed, it was Curtis who stumbled from his room first, his eyes already wild with dread.

"What's wrong?" he'd said. "Is somebody hurt?"

"I don't know," was Maxey's cowardly answer. And then she'd been saved by Janet's opening her door. "Inez is on the phone for you. She's crying."

"Oh Lordy," Janet said as she pushed past Maxey and ran down the hall, her flannel nightgown flapping around her white ankles.

When Janet began talking to Inez, Curtis leaned over her, his bony, pale body bare to the waist of his oil-spotted jeans. As soon as he pieced together what Inez was saying, he clutched his mother in a hug of such despair, Maxey had to turn away. Then he'd rushed upstairs for shirt and shoes before driving off into the night, probably to look for his friend one last time.

Now the kitchen clock read 2:47. Lance Chalmers had been dead for about two hours.

"I ought to go over there," Janet said, not moving.

Scotty patted her back. "There's nothing you can do."

"Inez—"

"Has her husband, and the minister. You can go over first thing tomorrow."

"Lance drove his convertible into a tree?" Maxey asked. "Do they know what happened?"

"He took the turn from the road into his own driveway too fast. Hit one of the big old maple trees in the corner square-on. Wasn't wearing a seat belt. Head and chest injuries."

"Inez and Richard must have heard the crash."

Janet nodded, eyes shut. "Thought it was a bomb. They reached him in minutes, but he was already gone."

"Why?" Maxey demanded. "Why would he run into the stupid tree right at his own house?"

Janet's eyes jumped open. "What do you mean, why? Some things just happen is all."

"Not an act of God, that's for sure," Scotty said bitterly.

"Maybe someone was chasing him," Maxey said. "Like the black truck did you, Janet."

"No." Janet straightened her shoulders and shook one finger at Maxey. "Don't you go inventing dark deeds and villains and turn this tragedy into some kind of mystery to be poked at and analyzed. The boy was driving too fast and had an accident. It was an accident. Understand?"

Maxey opened her mouth. Scotty gave her one quick shake of his head.

She stood up. "Anyone want more coffee?"

■

It had been stupid, drinking coffee while energized by the shock of Lance's death. Maxey lay on her back in bed, her eyes open in the dark. It was about 3:45. Curtis hadn't come home again, and she could bet that Janet, in her own bed up the hall, lay similarly sleepless.

Was Lance's death an accident? Or had he been killed for the same secret that might have killed Peggy Witter Burnell? Maxey envisioned a shapeless dark vehicle driven by a faceless, heartless someone who followed Lance home, failed to force him over an embankment or into a bridge rail, but herded him into his own lane, his own tree, at high speed.

Because—how did Ben's quotation go? If two are dead, three could keep a secret.

Maxey had no expectation that the authorities would call it anything but accidental death. She hoped above hope that it was.

At least if he'd been murdered, she could rule out Janet as his murderer. All Maxey's other suspects were probably at home asleep, too, but that would be impossible to verify.

She stared up at the invisible ceiling, and twin tracks of wetness trickled toward her ears. Had she killed Lance? Was it something she'd asked?

In the morning, they all looked like hell. Janet, in spite of the wig and eye shadow, moved around the kitchen with slow deliberation, like an octogenarian terrified of falling. Scotty sagged at the table, needing a shave, needing sleep, his eyes the same dull blue as his stonewashed denim shirt.

Maxey's eyes burned. She felt stiff and sore, as if she'd run into a wall. She sipped at a glass of orange juice that tasted vaguely metallic.

"Did Curtis get home all right?" she asked.

"About thirty minutes ago," Janet said. "I hope he can sleep most of the rest of the day. He was at the undertaker's. I couldn't believe that John Dorrance let him in to sit with the body."

"John must have seen how much Curtis needed to," Scotty said. "Needed to get good-bye out of his system."

Janet sniffed. "I'm going over to the Chalmerses'. You two will have to entertain yourselves today. You can really go to Heartland, if you've a mind to."

Scotty and Maxey exchanged guilty glances. They hadn't exactly lied about yesterday's activities. They told Janet they took a wrong turn, lost interest in fountains, and cruised around while trying to think of somewhere else to go. After getting a whiff of Scotty's breath, Janet probably decided they'd spent the afternoon in a tavern.

"Let me drive you over to Inez's," Maxey offered.

Her aunt gazed at her with obvious suspicion. "Why?"

"Because you're tired and preoccupied and shouldn't be driving."

"How will I get home again?"

"Phone and I'll come get you."

"You don't want to wait around all day for me to call."

"Sure I do."

"Jannie, let the girl drive you," Scotty said, settling it.

■

They found Inez trying to chop down the maple tree.

Maxey rolled Janet's car to a gentle stop in the driveway and Janet struggled out of the passenger seat, clucking and moaning in sympathy. Maxey followed her across grass that someone—probably Lance—had recently mowed. It glittered with a sprinkling of shattered glass.

"I know it's crazy," Inez said first. "But it makes me feel better, punishing this tree."

Her inexpert whacks had left a series of scratches up and down the trunk, none of them life-threatening. A far worse wound was the side facing the road, where the bark hung in splintered strips, exposing inner wood as pale as bloodless flesh.

Inez let the ax drop at her feet and wiped her face with the hem of her shirt. It looked like one of Richard's, a blue-and-white-striped dress shirt that reached the knees of her pink double-knit pants.

"If it's good therapy, I'd like to take a couple swings myself," Janet said. She embraced Inez, almost stepping on the ax, both of them staggering when they let go. "Come on, let's retire to the house. Where's Richard?"

"I don't know." She peered around the yard. "He's probably . . . I don't know."

"Come on." Janet clasped Inez by the elbow and drew her away. "Let's go sit awhile on your back porch."

Inez pulled free and looked pleadingly at Janet. "Would you go up to Lance's room and get him something nice to wear? The funeral director said for me to bring him some clothes, but I just don't think I can set foot in that room yet."

"Sure, hon."

"Is there anything I can do for you before I go?" Maxey asked.

"Maybe Inez would like you to take the clothes to the funeral parlor."

"I guess that would be all right," Inez said, wandering toward the tree again before Janet caught her arm and pointed her in the other direction.

"Come on, Inez. Come on, Maxey. Hut, two, three, four."

Maxey fell in on the other side of Inez, whose feet faltered to a full stop every few steps, then jerked into action again under Janet's patient coaching. Maxey followed them through the navy door into the cool, dim house. They walked through foyer, living room, and dining area, out to a sunporch that deserved to be on a magazine cover—all glass, white wicker furniture, and lusty green potted plants.

Inez dropped into a rocking chair and began to whip it back and forth. Her hands kneaded at the woven arms.

Janet studied her friend. "You're going to run right back outside the minute I leave you, aren't you?"

"It's probably either that or explode," Inez said.

"Maxey, you go get Lance's Sunday suit out of his closet," Janet ordered. "Shirt, tie, the works."

"Upstairs?"

"The only room up there. The steps are in the front hall, where we came in."

Maxey nodded and retraced their route, hounded by the sound of Inez's sneakers slapping the gray tile floor as she rocked.

The black wrought-iron stairway spiraled upward into the middle of an **A**-ceilinged room roughly the size of Maxey's entire apartment. The east wall was glass, divided by strips of oak, and it was open at the bottom, where there were louvers and screens. Three black hawk silhouettes warned flying birds away from the illusion of open sky. The view stretched for miles, an ocean of yellowing corn.

A water bed covered with a quilt—nothing fancy, just primary-colored squares—squatted in the northeast corner. Maxey imagined Lance lying there watching the stars and moon wheel by, thinking about cars and girls and what to be when he grew up.

Perhaps he'd kept a diary. Feeling bad about it, but not bad enough to stop herself, she walked to the bedside stand and checked the drawer. She found a blank memo pad, a Bic pen, an unopened box of cough drops, a pair of science fiction paperbacks, and enough loose nails, screws, pins, paper clips, and pushpins to batten down whatever might be loose.

Somewhere below, a door slammed, jarring Maxey back to her assignment. She looked around for the closet.

The west wall was all folding doors. The first pair she tried led into a chrome and glass bathroom strewn with towels and pajamas and socks.

The next two doors unfolded on closet space. Maxey skated the hangers along the rod until she found a white dress shirt. Draping it over her arm, she searched deeper, into a cluster of sport jackets and suits. While her compassionate self tried to decide which of these should be Lance's final change of clothes, her curious self felt in all the pockets. She discovered movie theater stubs, chewing gum, a loose button, video store receipts, a handkerchief, more screws and pins and paper clips.

She took out a gray suit and draped it over the shirt on her arm. Bending to the jumble of shoes on the floor, she sorted out two black loafers that seemed to match. She found a burgundy-and-blue pais-ley tie looped carelessly over an otherwise-empty hanger.

Does one wear underwear to one's funeral? Better to have it and not need it than the reverse. She moved to the next set of double doors, which concealed shelves of sweaters and drawers full of un-derwear and socks. Struggling not to drop anything she already car-ried, Maxey patted the layers of white T-shirts in the top drawer. The hard square shape she found was only a jeweler's box holding cuff links shaped like footballs.

Adding an undershirt to the stack of clothes on her arm, she slid out the next drawer down.

"What in the hell do you think you're doing?"

The voice, sudden and loud, almost made Maxey fling Lance's clothes above her head. Hugging them closer to her chest, she turned around.

Richard Chalmers stood, one foot in the room and the other on the top riser of the metal staircase, his face red with exertion and anger, his arms full of a gleaming brass and wood rifle.

"Inez asked me to—"

"Get out of my son's room."

"I'm only—"

He shifted the gun from resting across his chest to a more ready one-handed aim at the ceiling. "You should never have come to Gruder. Lance would still be alive if it wasn't for you."

"How can you say that? What have I done?"

"Snooped and pestered and drove us to distraction. Lance wasn't himself when he crashed into that tree. You can take that fact back to Colorado with you."

He swung the rifle to point at the windows on Maxey's left. His eyes glinted, daring her to argue with him further.

Trembling, she walked toward him, toward the stairs. He moved aside to let her by, reaching over her shoulder to wrest away the clothes she'd collected.

"Don't think I'd let him wear a thing you touched," he said.

As she circled down to the first floor, clinging to the rail as if on a heaving ship, she felt his spittle pepper the back of her neck.

She tottered across the foyer toward the living room.

"Take your aunt with you," he shouted.

Janet was kneeling beside Inez, who still plied the rocker as if her life depended on it. Both women looked up as Maxey stumbled on the threshold of the sunporch.

"Richard is very upset. He wants both of us to leave, Janet."

"Oh, pshaw. Don't mind him," Inez said. "He's always stirred up about something." She stared into space for a second before her mouth began to work, wordlessly at first and then on a high, thin wail. "Course, he's got a real reason this time."

Janet bent to her, clasping her hand, patting her back, crooning over her, then twitching around to frown at Maxey. "You go on. I'm staying."

"But—"

"I'm staying. I'll call you when I'm ready to go home."

Maxey fled, afraid she'd find Richard waiting in ambush between the back porch and the front door. But the living room and the foyer lay calm and clean and quiet. Stepping from the house to the sunny front stoop was like bursting to the surface from a deep, murky swamp.

■

"They didn't need his best clothes after all," Janet said. She had begged a ride home after dark with John Dorrance. "John couldn't fix his face up good enough for an open casket."

Maxey, curled in one corner of the couch with a poetry book she'd borrowed from Scotty, remembered Lance's handsome young face and flinched under a spasm of mental pain. Scotty, in the recliner in the corner, let his new map book fall shut. He could easily find his place again, Maxey thought, because he'd been staring at the same page ever since they'd sat down an hour ago.

Janet listed against the dining room archway. "The funeral's tomorrow morning."

"That soon? Isn't that rushing things?" Maxey asked.

"Richard wants to get it over with. No viewing hours. A mob of people isn't going to do Inez any good."

Scotty fought his chair upright and stepped out of it. "Come on to bed. You look out on your feet."

Janet didn't move. "Is Curtis home?"

"Not yet." Maxey emphasized the *yet,* a subtle reassurance that he would be home, safe and sound. Surely he would.

"Oh, Maxey, this is so awful for you."

"For me? I do feel awful, but I'm hardly—"

"Your lovely vacation, ending like this."

"A vacation seems pretty petty right now."

"Your plane leaves tomorrow. You'll miss the funeral."

"Well, yes, but I wouldn't do anyone any good by being there. In fact, Richard would probably throw me out of the cemetery if I showed up."

Scotty crooked his finger at Janet. "If you pass out down here, I'm not carrying you upstairs."

Janet moved toward Maxey instead. Bending over to embrace her, Janet whimpered against her cheek. "I'm sorry, sweetheart. I'm just so sorry."

Maxey, struggling straighter to meet her aunt halfway, patted awkwardly at her back. "You have plenty to worry about without worrying about me. Get some sleep now. Time heals all wounds, as they say."

"Oh yes, but—" Janet pulled away to look her in the eyes. "It leaves some awful scars."

In spite of Maxey's own need for sleep, sleep wouldn't come. She feared that insomnia was becoming a habit. She heard her aunt weeping at one o'clock, Curtis coming home at two o'clock, and a quiet rain beginning at three o'clock. And all the while, she tried to think who could have killed her mother besides who she feared had killed her mother.

■

The rain still hung around in the morning. Maxey's plane was scheduled to leave Omaha at 1:10. Allowing an hour to get there and an hour to check in, she should leave the farm around eleven o'clock. Packing her two suitcases, she felt defeated and depressed.

Lance, especially, tormented her.

Walking to the window overlooking the garden, Maxey leaned

against the frame and longed for a flash of insight, one tiny bit of reassurance that not everything was her fault.

A tapping on the bedroom door frame turned her around. Scotty stood there, natty in a navy pinstriped suit and vest. "Okay if I say my good-byes now before matters get hectic?"

She crossed the room, smiling. "Okay if I hug you before matters get hectic?"

"Dear heart, if you hug me, matters *will* get hectic."

Laughing, she did it anyway. His strong arms wrapped around her tightly. He smelled like soap.

"Lucky Janet," she mumbled against his shoulder pad.

"Huh?"

"Nothing." She stepped back.

"Are your bags ready to go downstairs?"

"Yes, but I can—"

He lifted them off the bed and led her down the back stairs.

Janet stood in the middle of the kitchen, attaching pearl studs to her ears. Her gray-blue dress swished as she rushed to Maxey for a perfunctory hug.

"Scotty and I have to go. Are you leaving now?"

"It's too early to leave for the airport." Maxey looked across Janet's shoulder at the breakfast dishes clogging the sink. "Do you mind if I hang around here a while longer?"

"Do what you want. Just pull the back door to. You don't need to lock it, I guess." She paused, apparently reconsidering that. Then she shrugged. "I'm sorry Curtis isn't here to say good-bye."

Maxey hadn't seen Curtis since the night of Lance's death. Wherever and however he was mourning for his friend, it wasn't at home.

Janet grabbed up her purse and a plastic rain bonnet from the kitchen table. "Isn't this the classic day for a funeral, though? You got the umbrella, Scotty?" She bustled onto the back porch.

Scotty raised one palm at Maxey. "There's an old Scottish saying, 'His absence is good company.' Yours won't be." The door banged shut behind him.

Maxey watched them drive out the lane. She pushed up the sleeves of her tan sweatshirt and set to work on the dishes. The windows were alive with random fat raindrops. Thunder trundled along the horizon.

It was the first time she'd been alone in the house. It settled around her, creaking and tapping under the weight of the wind and rain. Once, Maxey held her breath, hands dripping suds as she listened to footsteps on the back porch. When no one came in, she screwed her courage to the sticking point, as Scotty and Mr. Shakespeare would have said, and went to see. It was the reclusive kittens, tumbling one another dizzy.

Dishes finished, Maxey checked the wall clock, then strolled aimlessly through the dining room, the living room, and on through the double doors to the front hall. She gazed up the stairwell, turned, and wandered into the living room again.

Janet's ladder of potted plants yearned toward the window, every leaf perky and shining. Maxey ran a finger around the orange clay lip of one pot. Somewhere she'd read that sounds might be trapped in the grooves of ancient pottery. If someone had shouted or a dog had barked near the potter while he worked, the vessel might have recorded those.

If only this room could play back sounds.

She had a few minutes to waste. Why not spend them retracing her mother's last moments?

She returned to the stairwell, took the steps two at a time, strode to her room—her mother's room—and perched on the side of the bed. The rain suddenly stopped.

All right, it's afternoon. I've had a headache, and now I've wakened from a nap. I get up. Maybe I look out the window. There's Janet in the strawberry patch with two little kids, Curtis and Lance. She's bending over to pick, straddling a row. The boys are squatted down, scratching at bug bites and eating every other berry.

What do I do next?

I ought to go pick my share for tonight's shortcake.

So I walk into the hall, like this, down to use the bathroom. Then I go into the hall again, and I turn left again. Because why would I go down the front stairs if I'm going out the back door to the garden?

So then why do I go down the front stairs?

Because I hear someone at the front door. I turn right and walk down the stairs. Let this person in. We talk a little bit.

About what, damn it?

Maxey rubbed at her forehead, feeling a real headache coming on.

Let's say the visitor is Sophie Otis. She's accusing me of sneaking around with her husband. But I wouldn't do that—not to someone whose life I'd saved. And if I did cheat with Dennis, Sophie wouldn't accuse me of it—because I saved her life.

Rewind this scene back to where the killer comes in the front door. Is it Tommy Coffman? Maybe he's here to apologize for scaring Janet this morning. Checking to see if I'm okay. Do I have a bruise on my face from a sisterly slap? Was Tommy really coming on to Janet, and is he back to finish the job? But she's outside and here I am, any port in a storm, so to speak.

No. Tommy doesn't have that much passion for anything that doesn't have a motor.

Francis, then? Has he come to pester for a date? Is he getting angry at the constant rejection? He'd have to be crazy to shoot somebody over an unsatisfactory social calendar.

How about Richard Chalmers? Does he want to start an affair with me or end one? Do I know something about him that threatens his marriage, his lifestyle, his reputation? Am I blackmailing him? What does he say that scares me so much I run upstairs for the rifle?

Because if anything is clear, it's that I, Peggy Burnell, had to bring the rifle down from the junk room. Who else would have known it was there?

Maxey covered her face with her hands. Who else indeed?

But why? What was the motive?

Maxey guessed there must be a thousand reasons an older sister might have for wanting to kill her younger sister—beginning with her birth.

"I'm going to get more empty quart boxes," Janet would have said to the boys. And they wouldn't have noticed how long she was gone. They probably wouldn't even have noticed that she wasn't in the garden when the shot was fired. She could have rushed back around the house to them, asked them what the noise was, then run into the house again, and they would never have noticed the questionable sequence of events.

Unless, of course, one of them had noticed. Perhaps that was Lance's awful secret.

No!

Maxey leapt up and paced the thin carpet, hands clenched at her side.

The killer must have been a transient.

She marched to the foot of the stairs and willed herself to begin a new scenario, one in which her mother heard a noise downstairs, someone thumping around and muttering drunkenly to himself, so she got the rifle out of the closet.

That's the sort of thing a woman might do if she was frightened and not thinking straight. Provide her own murder weapon for someone stronger to take away from her.

Maxey crossed back into the living room as a finger of sun touched the floor and as quickly faded.

She could imagine her mother carrying the heavy gun in here, trying to hold it steady while the barrel weaved at the ceiling. She'd be shouting at the intruder to get out of the house. His arm and hand would reach to yank it out of her grip. She'd stumble backward, eyes wide, seeing the hand work the bolt, seeing the barrel swing up, seeing nothing forever.

Maxey started and looked at her watch. There was still plenty of time before her plane left, but she couldn't stay in this house a moment longer.

15

. . .

Maxey risked getting lost by driving west instead of east and taking the first road south, all to avoid going straight through Gruder, where the funeral procession would be on its way to the cemetery about now. The unfamiliar gravel road seemed to unroll through the cornfields forever, but finally it intersected a paved highway, and she spotted the sign for U.S. 30. Breathing a sigh of relief, she turned east.

The Escort rattled almost as much on the concrete highway as it had on the gravel. Wind hissed through the hole in the back window, blowing the smell of rotted flowers into the front seat.

The rain clouds still wavered between going and staying, intermittently dampening the windshield with a fine mist. Maxey hoped it didn't get worse. In addition to the rest of the car's infirmities, the windshield wipers didn't work.

She slowed a little for Ames. The metal grain-storage bins strung out along the road were different degrees of shiny, youngest to oldest.

She couldn't shake the feeling that she was running away.

Okay. Nebraska wasn't a total waste of time. So I didn't nail my mother's killer. I did find my father. Of course, strictly speaking, that was in Colorado.

A red-winged blackbird sailed out of the side ditch and back in again. A sign invited her to visit the Nebraska Softball Hall of Fame.

I saw some interesting sights. And Scotty—I wouldn't have met Scotty if I hadn't come to Nebraska. Maybe if I keep my appearance up and learn how to cook, I'll be blessed with a Scotty in my old age. I've got to buy myself a good book of quotations—once I've saved some money again after spending it all on the Chateau Chaminade.

Another sign told her she was five miles from Fremont. A spate of rain hit the windshield, but before she could slow down, it ended—like being spit on by Richard Chalmers.

She moaned under a sweep of regret. Poor Lance. Poor all his family and friends.

But damn it, poor me, too. I'm the one whose mother was murdered. I'm the one who asked reasonable questions that met with unreasonable attempts to scare me off—red water, black trucks, dirty tricks. A Grudergate.

Her giggle sounded more like a whimper.

Secrets. At least one secret, deep and exceedingly dark. A secret to die for. How does it go? "Three may keep a secret—if two of them are dead." Mom and Lance, and killer makes three.

Just ahead, a cement truck lumbered onto the highway in the Fremont-bound lane, and she automatically let up on the accelerator.

How about four? Can four keep a secret if three of them are dead?

The headache that had been flirting with her all morning settled behind her eyes. She kneaded her left eyebrow.

Lance would never have kept any secret from Curtis, no matter how deep and dark. Even if he'd tried to hold it back, it would have sneaked out sometime, somewhere.

The cement truck turned off again, but Maxey didn't accelerate. She was too busy picturing Curtis trying to drive off his grief—literally—taking a curve too fast, following his friend into eternity. And, as in Lance's death, who would know whether Curtis had left the road all on his own or been forced into the smashup by someone piling secret upon secret?

Without even glancing at her watch, Maxey bumped the Escort into the side road behind the cement truck, swept a U-turn, looked both ways on Highway 30, and headed back toward Gruder.

■

Curtis's Mustang sat in the barnyard. Maxey couldn't believe her luck. Slamming the door of her own car, she ran through the wet grass and up on the back porch.

She stopped in the middle of the kitchen and listened. "Curtis?"

The cat prowled out of the dining room and yawned with her whole head. Footsteps sounded overhead.

Maxey walked through the house and up the front stairs. "Curtis?" The door to his room stood halfway open. She leaned to peer inside.

He'd made a small mountain of belongings on the floor at the foot of his unmade bed. Maxey noted a rolled sleeping bag, a military green backpack, a red windbreaker, and a sheaf of rolled, rubber-banded posters before his sharp voice drew her attention across the room. "What do you want now?"

He'd just ducked out of the depths of his closet. Both hands were full of shoes. He shot her an annoyed glance before tossing them on the bed and returning to the closet.

Maxey called after him. "If I took a wild guess, I'd say you were going somewhere for an extended period."

"Duh." He stalked to the bed again to dump an armful of shirts.

"Does your mom know?"

"You're a reporter all right. Asking obvious, dumb questions."

"Where is she?"

"On her way to the Chalmerses'. To put on a big spread for all the mourners. As if a funeral makes everyone hungry."

"It's just a custom. It comforts people to feel that life goes on, in spite of the loss."

The muscles in his jaw flexed. He threw a battered suitcase on the bed and began to pack.

"Why are you going? Where will you go?"

"I've got friends besides Lance. I hate this house. Flat-out hate it."

"Curtis, I'm afraid for you. I think you know something that someone might kill you to protect."

"You think too damned much." His packing consisted of wadding and jamming everything. The shoes went in helter-skelter, dirty soles and all.

Maxey felt the need to talk fast and wished she knew what to say. "You know the same secret Lance knew. I'm sure you do. It may be why he's dead."

"He's dead because he misjudged how fast he was going when he hit the drive. Maybe he had a beer on the way home."

"There was alcohol involved?"

"No. I don't know. The point is, he was careless. I'll be careful. Unless I decide life sucks too much."

"Curtis!"

"Maxey!" he mocked. He snatched up the backpack and shrugged into it. Then he latched the suitcase and swung it off the bed, its sides leaking scraps of clothing that hadn't been crammed in well enough. "Look out. Coming through."

She backed into the hall. "You know who murdered my mother, don't you? Tell me, or tell the sheriff, before the killer comes for you."

Curtis paused in the doorway, the suitcase dragging his thin shoulder toward the floor, his other arm crushing the sleeping bag to his chest. He glanced at her, then stared the length of the hall, his eyes bleak and far too old.

"You think you're so smart." His lips compressed as he fought not to cry. "Trust me. Lance wasn't murdered, and I won't be, either." Shoving past her, he strode toward the stairs. Halfway down, he shouted back, "You might want to watch your own ass, though."

Maxey slumped against the door frame, feeling futile. After a minute, the Mustang fired up and gunned past the house to the road.

Straightening, Maxey checked her watch. She'd still make her plane, even allowing for ten minutes of arguing with the rental company over their misused Escort.

As she trotted downstairs to the kitchen, she heard another car stop in the barnyard. Scotty came striding in the back door.

"Shouldn't you be on your way to Omaha?" he asked, loosening his tie and whipping off his jacket.

"Yes, I was just leaving. How was the funeral?"

"A mob of people, half of them kids. Sad. Sad." He walked to the sink and drew a drink of water. Maxey noticed that he held up the glass and looked through it before drinking.

"Curtis is running away from home," she said.

He grunted. Then he turned around to look her in the eye. "So am I."

"What?"

"I'm tired of wasting my sympathy on lies when there's too much real misery in the world. I'm getting out before I get accused of something I didn't do."

"What!"

"I don't know. Forging checks, maybe. Come on, Maxey. Don't look at me like that. It's not the end of civilized society."

"It might be the end of Janet's. She loves you."

"You think so? My guess is, I'm convenient to have around. A handyman and bed warmer."

Maxey held to the back of the chair she'd occupied while enjoying so many home-cooked meals. "What lies?"

Scotty set the empty glass on the counter. "The one about your father killing your mother. And how he attempted rape. Tommy Coffman's attempted rape. Half the male population in Dodge County's attempted rape. You want me to go on? How about the black truck trying to run her into the bridge?"

"That was a lie?"

"I can't prove it, but I surely do doubt that episode existed anywhere except in Janet's fertile imagination. Her own car worked fine when I tried to start it, so why would she want to take your rental except to make it sound like the alleged truck was after you instead. So you'd be scared off your hunt."

Hearing her suspicions put into audible words made Maxey want to cover her ears.

Scotty turned toward the back stairs. "She's telling the truth about one thing, Maxey. There's no point in your digging around, trying to turn up clues. If you did find any, you wouldn't like where they pointed. You'd cover them up as fast as you could bury them."

She crossed the room to grab his sleeve. "Scotty, do you know who the murderer is?"

He smiled mirthlessly back at her. "Not for a fact. I've got a robust hunch, though."

"Tell me," she said, though she still fought the urge to clamp her hands over her ears.

He patted her arm before putting his back to her again. "No. If I'm wrong, it could cause a world of hurt."

"Damn it!" Maxey smacked the wall with her palm, and pain surged up to her shoulder.

"Go fly a plane," Scotty called as he ran up the stairs.

Instead, she went to sit by the table, rubbing her arm and listening to the faint sounds of Scotty packing.

He was back in five minutes, his brown suitcase as scruffy as Curtis's, but without any of the stuffing leaking out. He frowned to see Maxey. "Well?"

"Just tell me this much. Do you think Janet lied when she said she was in the garden with the two boys when the shot was fired?"

Scotty opened the door, waited for the incoming cat to sidle out of his way, and shuffled out on the porch. He leaned back to answer before the door closed. "Yes."

"Oh God," Maxey muttered, watching him lift his bag through the rear door of the Bronco. "Oh God, oh God, oh God."

After she heard the engine start and saw Scotty's out-the-window wave, Maxey looked at her watch again. If there weren't any patrol cars between here and Omaha, she could still make her flight. She quick-stepped toward the door, paused, and turned to consider the table.

Did Scotty leave Janet a note? Did Curtis? No matter what she's done, she'll worry about them if there's no note.

Finding a pencil and a pad of scratch paper by the telephone, Maxey scribbled a pair of sentences: "C. and S. have both left (separately) for I don't know where for I don't know how long. By left, I mean bags and all. Love, Maxey."

Making a face, she balled up the paper, rewrote the note leaving out *love,* and weighted it to the table with Scotty's water glass.

Hearing gravel crunch under tires, she craned to look out the window over the sink. Her heart gave a little hitch of apprehension as a big black truck rolled to a hard, rocking stop. The driver's door popped open and Janet struggled out.

Feeling like a fox caught in an empty henhouse, Maxey held the door wide for her. Bustling past, Janet headed for a high cupboard and began pulling out unopened packs of paper plates and cups.

"All the people who felt cheated out of a viewing showed up at the house. Mostly kids. We've got enough food for an army, but we're running out of dishes and such. Shouldn't you be halfway to the airport?"

"Yes. How's Inez holding up?"

"Too well. She's smiling and playing the queen, and any minute I expect to see her blow up and scatter. Even us strong women can only bear so much."

Agreeing, Maxey glanced at the note on the table.

Janet snapped open a grocery bag and began to stuff it with the disposable plates. "Do you know what Inez told me? I can't decide whether to believe it or not. She says she made up her cancer. Says she just pretended to be feeling so bad so that Richard would feel sorry for her and treat her better. Doesn't that just tell you more than you want to know about him? I hope it's true—that she's not sick, I mean. I don't know why she'd lie to me about it. A person shouldn't lie about something that important."

"But lying about murder is okay?" Maxey stepped in front of her aunt and gently grasped both of her wrists. "Please. Look me in the eyes and tell me. Where were you when the shot killed my mother?"

Janet's wine-colored bangs lay plastered by perspiration against her forehead. She'd chewed off all her lipstick. Her face seemed to become older, become real, under Maxey's stare.

Janet gritted her teeth before she answered, her eyes steady and determined. "I was in the garden picking strawberries."

Sighing, Maxey let go of her hands and stepped back. "I thought so."

Janet jammed another package of cups into the sack. "This isn't healthy, this obsession of yours. You should learn to let go of things you can't change. Like that saying, Grant me the serenity to change what I can and forget about what I can't. Or however it goes." She forced a chuckle. "I sound like Scotty."

"I can't change Mom's death. I *can* change the injustice of my father being accused of it."

"Oh, nobody believed he did it but me, anyway. If that's all you want, I withdraw the charge. Dee didn't kill Peggy. Satisfied?" Janet jerked open a drawer and stirred through it before slamming it. "I swear, if I'd known how difficult you would be, I'd never have encouraged you to come to Gruder. I can't say I blame Richard for thinking you're partly responsible for Lance's accident."

Hugging herself, Maxey tried to control her voice. "Don't you blame me for Lance. I'm not the one who burdened him with a secret. I didn't kill Peggy Burnell."

"You're just jabbering now. If you miss your plane, don't come back here for the night. You've worn out your welcome."

Maxey could see Janet's hands trembling as badly as her own. It felt as if the house were shaking.

Her voice rattled out of her throat. "I've figured it out, Janet. I think I know how my mother died."

They eyed each other across the room. Then Janet casually reached around to the knife rack and selected the biggest, nastiest butcher knife. "Get out."

"If you're going to stab someone, you don't hold the knife overhand like that. Hold it at your waist with the blade up, so you can jab upward and hook the victim's vitals."

"Don't you mock me, Maxine Diane. Don't you misjudge me."

"I think you're a talented liar, Janet. I don't think you could murder anyone."

"You think I shot my sister to death."

"I didn't say that."

Janet's hot pink face gradually drained to pasty white. "All right. You win. I'll tell you the absolute truth. I did shoot Peggy." She set the knife carefully on the counter, dug into her dress pocket, and brought out a much-used handkerchief. "But it was self-defense. She'd got the rifle and was accusing me of trying to steal Dee away from her. We struggled, and the gun went off." Janet blew her nose.

"How could it be self-defense? The shot was fired from ten feet away."

Janet threw her hands into the air. "I can't remember. It all happened so fast. I guess she fell back and I fell back and the gun went off."

"An accidental shooting? In self-defense? I don't think you would have burdened two little kids with that kind of secret for the rest of their lives. I think you swore Lance and Curtis to secrecy to protect someone. And there's only one person I can imagine you wanting to protect that much."

"No." She shook her head so hard, dust motes flew in the brightening room. She snatched up the knife again. "It was me."

Maxey knew she shouldn't say more, but she couldn't stop herself. "It was Curtis."

"That's ridiculous and you know it. He was only a baby then."

"He was eight. Just the right age to be fascinated by guns."

Janet's face crimped into a mask of grief. She drew out a chair and slumped at the table, one hand over her eyes, the other gripping the knife, blade up, the way Maxey had advised her.

Maxey's own legs wouldn't support her anymore. She scraped another chair out and fell into it. "You were in the garden picking strawberries. Curtis and Lance were in the house, supposedly watching TV or something. But they'd brought the rifle down from the junk room, and when my mother surprised them by suddenly appearing in the hall doorway, Curtis reflexively clutched the rifle. Squeezed the trigger."

Janet didn't answer. Her weeping was quiet and genuine.

Maxey traced the yellow oilcloth pattern with one finger. "Monday night, I came downstairs and surprised the boys in the living room. They looked at me like I was a ghost. I thought Curtis said something about 'view,' but now I'm sure it was 'déjà vu.' "

Janet continued to cry, her shoulders hunched with pain.

"You lied to protect Curtis, and you made him and Lance lie, too," Maxey said. "Your intentions were good. It might not have been the right thing to do, but I can understand why you did it. All except your accusing Dee. If you hadn't lied about Dee, I wouldn't have launched my own investigation. Maybe." Maxey got to her feet and backed carefully toward the door.

Janet peeked out between her fingers. "What are you going to do?" she asked in a thick, frightened voice.

"Fly home to Colorado. Keep your secret. What I'm not going to do is bear all the responsibility for Lance's accident. If he ran into the tree while he was preoccupied, thinking about this family, then we have to divide the guilt three ways. Four, if you include Mom. Then again, maybe he ran into the tree because he'd had a fight with his girlfriend, or because he'd been out too late and fell asleep. I intend to take your advice and have the serenity to know I can't change it, whatever caused his death."

Janet dabbed at her mouth and nose with the handkerchief. "You aren't going to tell anyone about us? About Curtis?"

"No." Maxey's legs felt like overcooked noodles. "It's a secret among us three."

Janet studied the tip of the knife in her quaking hand. Then she laid it gently on the table.

Maxey tottered across to the back door. "Or maybe it's a four- or five-way secret. I'm guessing Richard Chalmers knows. And maybe Inez, too."

Janet groaned.

As Maxey swung the door open and stepped out, she thought she saw her aunt reach for the Dear Janet note. She accelerated off the porch.

In the Escort, she circled around the Chalmerses' truck and sped toward the road, feeling certain it was for the last time. It had taken her ten years to work up the enthusiasm for this visit to the home place. She couldn't imagine ever wanting to come again—or Janet wanting her to.

She drove too fast through Gruder—all four tires airborne over the railroad tracks and a hard landing on the other side. As she flogged the car toward North Bend, she eyed the relentless progress of the dashboard clock. She wasn't going to check in with any time to spare, but she could still make her flight.

Having resolved to concentrate on her driving and not to think about anything or anyone, she got as far as Fremont before she broke her resolution and thought of Scotty. A red light brought her to a rocking stop. Fingers drumming on the steering wheel, she wondered where he'd driven to by now.

The green light released her. She followed traffic through downtown, past the justice building.

It would be so great to be home, especially now that Clark Dumpty was out of the *Regard* on his big flat head.

"I dote on his very absence." William Shakespeare.

The idea felt exactly like a lightbulb flaring on. She reached to her shoulder bag on the passenger seat and felt inside till she found her notebook, all the while scanning ahead for the blue and chrome of a public phone booth.

She found one lurking at the curb beside a filling station, which reminded her that she was supposed to return the Escort with a full tank. She snorted. She was also supposed to return it in one piece.

Parking beside the booth, she hopped out, found the right page in the notebook, and dialed the number. After six rings, as Maxey began to feel disappointment seep in, the telephone clicked three times and emitted a curt hello.

She leaned into the open booth, forefinger plugging her free ear against the racketing traffic a few yards away. "Scotty?"

A scrabbling static ensued. "Yes," he finally confirmed.

"This is Maxey. Where are you?"

"I don't know. On seventy-seven. Bypassing Lincoln. Can you hear me okay? Dang. This isn't as easy as it looks. Where are you?"

"Not close enough to Omaha. Scotty, please come work at the *Regard*. What I'd really like is for you to go into partnership with me."

"Be careful what you ask for."

"You haven't got any place better to go, right? Come to Boulder and decide."

"What I have to decide right now is whether to let this semi squeeze me off this on-ramp."

"Think about it. Seriously."

The phone squawked and went dead. She hoped the disconnect didn't signify the semi had won.

She wouldn't have time to explain anything to the rental people, wouldn't have time to check her bags at the front desk, wouldn't have time to use the rest room. Still, she could catch her flight if she parked in an unloading zone, dashed straight to the gate, and crossed her legs till the captain shut off the seat-belt sign so she could stampede to the lavatory.

■

She dropped the Escort's key on the counter in front of a woman with an orange scarf knotted artfully around her shoulder, then turned to sprint away.

"Bill me. It's parked out front," Maxey shouted, the two suitcases banging her knees with every step.

The scarfed lady called after her. "You can't leave it out front. That'll cost you twenty dollars extra!"

It was hard to laugh and run at the same time.